ENTOPIA

ENTOPIA

ENT-
From the Greek word *entom,*
meaning "insect"

-TOPIA
From the Greek word *topos,*
meaning "place"

ENTOPIA

REVOLUTION OF THE ANTS

RAD ZDERO

Illustrations by William A. Treble

CAPSTONE
FICTION

WATERFORD, VIRGINIA

Entopia: Revolution of the Ants

Published in the U.S. by:
Capstone Publishing Group LLC
P.O. Box 8
Waterford, VA 20197

Visit Capstone Fiction at
www.capstonefiction.com

Cover design by YellowCanaryDesign.com
Interior illustrations © 2008 by William A. Treble
Map © 2008 by Rad Zdero
Author photo © 2007 by Rad Zdero

ISBN: 978-1-60290-004-2

To the
Pale White Ant

acknowledgments

My thanks go out to these fine folks for their helpful feedback in the creation of this tale: my dear sister Jelica Zdero, who continues to be one of my best friends and muses as we pursue our common cause; my close chum Geoff Leung, whose razor-sharp mind always cuts away bits of my dullness through our marathon conversations; my fellow pilgrim Fred Duquette, whose passion for true philosophy and Shakespeare has brought me fresh perspective; and my co-labourer Kim Butler, whose love of fun and language is infectious.

PANGAEA
(prior to The Third War of the West)

N
W E
S

Darktree

Waters of
Darktree

Greenwood

Bloodflower

Stone of
Greenwood

← Entmerika

No Ant's Land

Old Entgora

Field
of
Yellowgrass

Hill of
Fatgrass

New Entgora

water
trench
of N.E.

Exodus
Tree

Colonies
of
Entopia

"ENTOPIA"
by
Rad Zdero

1

the new wind

A new wind was blowing that day in Pangaea. This was during the Old World days when the land was undivided, before the falling of the great floodwaters that destroyed almost all life. The wind was blowing in a new direction and was possessed of a strange warmth. Nothing else seemed unbefitting and, otherwise, things were quite ordinary.

It was the kind of wind—a mere breeze in fact—that caused Gazer to stop, put down her crumb of food, raise her head, and wiggle her long antennae around in a controlled chaos. She was ever the one to stop and stare at something—the midday light, the winged beasties that flew high overhead, the trees, other ants—and was aptly named.

Was it the breath of the Outside Beast that she felt? Was it one of those hated, long-tongued fiends who, legend has it, once raided her colony's anthill and consumed hundreds of her fellow ants?

Dread filled her head, and her limbs were shot through with painful electricity. *Oh dear!* she thought. *This is certainly not a worthy way to come to my end of days!*

Although she was unafraid to die by being inhaled by an Outside Beast, her grandest hope, rather, was to meet her end in the same heroic manner as did one of the first ants of ancient times not forgotten.

The old tales speak of the Great Ant coming countless

seasons ago from the Great Anthill, which was far and away in the direction of the rising of the Great Light and beyond the Great Water.

It is said that the Great Ant led a long line of ants on a perilous journey—for good reason was it called the Great March—across the open plain to begin a new colony. It was unclear if this was done of their own accord or because she and her fellow pilgrims were cast out from their home.

The journey unfolded soundly and no ant lives were lost... that is, until they faced the vastness of the Great Water.

On two prospects did the ants ponder long. Either they could sojourn there for a time in the open, risking attack from beasts. Or they could attempt to return to the Great Anthill and risk the perils of beast and terrain and weather that a second journey would surely bring. They had come to an impasse. Their path lay hidden to them.

While under the glare of the day's blistering light, a third way flashed like lightning across the mind of the Great Ant. But the scheme was too risky and too unfamiliar. Would the others understand? Would the others follow her course? Would she be abandoned for thinking un-antlike thoughts and doing un-antlike things?

The Great Ant—tugging at the courage that dwelt within and impassioned by the vision of starting a new colony—did something no ant had dared to ever conceive.

She stepped into the water.

The braver of her travelling companions did she call upon to do the same, such that a large host perished. The ruins of their drowned bodies formed a bridge over which the remaining grief-stricken ant line did pass into freedom, carrying with it the renewed hope of a new colony and the memory of the visionary self-sacrifice of the Great Ant.

And so the tale is told and retold. There was no reason to question the story since most ants, including Gazer, embraced the truth of it. A peculiar few thought it a strange, and perhaps unbelievable, thing that an ant would act so oddly and do something so original. Although worker ants knew something of these matters, it was only the Queen and her inner circle that were privy to the words of the Chronicles of Entgora, giving them a true knowledge of the colony's history. This deeper wisdom, however, was forbidden to ordinary ants like Gazer. Yet, what trifles the workers knew, they faithfully believed.

Gazer brought to remembrance the rhyme she learned as a young hatchling from the older worker ants, being taught in turn by their elders, and so on, back through time out of mind. The young ones would grasp each other's antennae and dance and leap about in a play circle, chanting their little song:

Hatchling, hatchling, tiny ant
Hear and tell, listen well
Hatchling, hatchling, tiny ant
To the story

Hatchling, hatchling, tiny ant
The Great Ant left her hill
Hatchling, hatchling, tiny ant
Marching bravely

Hatchling, hatchling, tiny ant
The Great Ant had to stop
Hatchling, hatchling, tiny ant
At the Great Water

Hatchling, hatchling, tiny ant
The Great Ant jumped in first
Hatchling, hatchling, tiny ant
And saved the daughters

It was this kind of noble and courageous and, yet, unusual ant that Gazer desired to emulate when she reached her own end of days. And being eaten by an Outside Beast during a routine food expedition was not her idea of a remarkably noble end.

As fortune would dictate, no big vile beast was in sight of Gazer's glassy many-chambered eyes or breathing its sickly breath across the sensitive hairs of her back. It was just the wind, although odd in its pleasantness and carrying with it a scent of anticipation.

Gazer the black worker ant, now free of fear, reached down, picked up her ball of food once again, and squeezed her belly against the ground to resume the goopy liquid trail that other ants would gladly follow to the treasure of food she had discovered.

She then marched back home.

2

the daily fare

As Gazer drew near to her home, she passed under the long shadow cast against the ground by her native anthill, named Entgora. The dirt grey hill, which to her was a mountain many times as high as her own frame, gleamed in the light like a smooth pointy cone. The vast mazework of the hill, however, largely lay buried deep underground, where life teemed and activity was endless. The anthill was many-

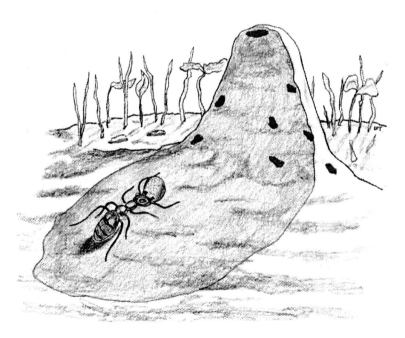

layered, and its reach was deep and broad into the expanse of the earth. Many chambers of sundry types did abound. Some for sleep and rest. Others for holding unsavoury lawbreakers. Larger caverns were used for stocking of food, while still others housed twigs and stones and leaves. So great was this labyrinth home that, now and then, ants just might lose their way and wander for some time until such time that they picked up just the right scent to lead them to just where they were going to go before they got lost in the first place.

As Gazer merged with a line of other returnees into one of the holeways in the side of the hill, she was approached quickly by a much larger soldier ant with antennae thrust towards her.

"In the name of the Queen! Stop! State your affairs!" the soldier yelled.

Though it was the custom of the soldiers to inspect every ant returning to the hill, it unsettled Gazer and the other workers each time. How could one not be at least mildly frightened, when a much larger and stronger soldier ant rushed towards you with interrogating eyes and snapping jaws, swinging large stick-like antennae each time one returned home from simply doing one's antish duty on the outside? These soldiers were nicknamed Pokers, because they were habitually poking and prodding others.

"Oh, I'm a worker ant just returning from a food hunt. I'm off to make this delivery to a food storage area. Have a nosh? It hasn't spoilt, really," Gazer replied nervously.

For a few brief moments, the soldier ant's antennae caressed the surface of Gazer's roundish head and long slender antennae, ensuring that she in fact had the familiar smell and taste and touch of a worker ant returning home and not of some hostile intruder. Yet, this was their habit and nothing to be troubled over. And, after the brief inspection, the soldier ant was satisfied.

"Carry on, little worker!" the soldier bellowed, moving

quickly on to the other ants still to be examined. Gazer was allowed to pass to make her delivery.

As she moved swiftly through the lightless tunnels to one of the chief food caverns, she passed many others streaming in the opposite direction, greeting those she knew with "Hullo!" and "Chipper day!" She felt glad that with diligence was she serving her Sovereign.

The old Queen was the unquestioned ruler of Entgora and the only fertile female ant in the entire colony, which numbered some one hundred and twenty thousand ants strong. Workers and soldiers, though, were sterile females because of a scent the Queen dispatched throughout the hill. For many a season she would faithfully lay thousands of eggs from which would spring forth the next generation of workers, soldiers, males, and one or more new future Queens, commonly called Princesses. The much smaller winged male ants were forbidden to return to the anthill after having served a Princess's reproductive needs. They did their duty and were no longer needed. They were then exiled and were required to fend for themselves on the outside. They usually died several days later. A Princess, now impregnated, would leave the hill and seek out a new place to birth her own colony, having for its citizens her newborns.

Or so Gazer was told. She had never personally seen the physical act of mating. And neither had any ordinary worker ant, as it was unlawful to witness such an event. It was sacred and not to be disturbed by curious onlookers. Yet the imaginations of some workers were so bemused at the promising details of such mysteries and the reasons for their secrecy, that they would tell and retell the same humorous yarns about breeding.

One of the most wily of tales was that of Stumpleg, the puniest and most timid male ant that ever did live, and Wombella, a grotesquely large, unattractive, and unseemly

Princess. Soon after mating, Stumpleg's life became so unpleasant because of the irksomely demanding female that he left the colony to perish alone—rather than bear another moment in her dreadful company—by flinging himself from the top of a quite large boulder and refusing to flap his wings. And the act was so unsatisfying and anticlimactic for Wombella that she flew far away to rid her womb of any sign of her now fertilized eggs, unwittingly giving birth to a new ant colony. Neither told any other ant about their brief encounter. And the secrets of breeding remain so to this day, or so it is said. It was a wry tale to be sure, Gazer thought, but not a jolly one.

Gazer soon arrived at one of the large food caverns. From these central spots, food was hauled by worker ants to others in the colony throughout the complex mazework of the anthill. At other times, workers out on food forages would fetch their bounty and share it straightaway with others upon their return home.

As she reached the storage area, Gazer noticed her old friend Tenspeed among the crowd. They had come from the same brood of eggs and so were of the same age.

"Miss Gazer! Miss Gazer! Throw me a glance."

"Oh! Tenspeed! How are you, my dear friend?"

"Ah, not so bad, truth be told, truth be told, and I've got so many things to do today and I'm just dropping off this bit of victual—small as it is—and then I have to run off to help with some repair projects and then I have to zip over, indeed, and take out some garbage to the trash pile outside! And yourself? And yourself?"

"The same. Which brings to mind the…" Gazer started to say.

"Well, must be off, must be off," Tenspeed blurted, soon out of sight before Gazer could finish her words.

"Always dashing off somewhere to do something," Gazer mused in delight as she watched Tenspeed—named so because she sped along as if she had ten legs instead of six—scamper away lickety-split through the mouth of one of the tunnels.

Gazer left the storage grotto after depositing her bit of food and carried on with her next duty. Workers like Gazer and Tenspeed at times were given orders from their masters to focus on one task that day, usually either food collection or distribution, repairs or construction, or possibly rubbish removal from the hill. On some days, their tasks were varied and pleasant, which was always a welcome treat. Yet, now and then, workers given the charge to repair damaged regions of the hill brought on by weather calamities were crushed accidentally or sacrificed by design. Denial of self was needful for tasks of such importance.

The Queen directed the affairs of the entire Entgoran colony through a disciplined and highly regimented ant-over-ant system. She herself did no work. Yet she was the fountain of all life and was referred to as Mother. She, along with her select inner circle of soldier ants, formally known as Royal Soldiers, was brought the choicest of foods and provided with the best living quarters one could possibly hope to find inside the hill. The Royal Soldiers were mischievously nicknamed Shouters by the worker ant class because they tended to give out orders rather loudly.

The Queen and her Royal Soldiers enjoyed their pleasures, power, and prestige, and were intent on maintaining such a scheme. All seemed to be functioning well. Every ant knew their place. Every ant knew well their duties. Every ant knew to whom they owed their allegiance. Everything was in order. Everything was as it should be. And no ant murmured openly.

In truth, the Queen was rarely seen in person by the average worker ant, including Gazer and most soldier ants. The mere mention of her in polite conversation stirred up a kind of awe. It was quite conceivable that a worker ant could labour from birth to her end of days without having any personal knowledge of the Royal One.

Gazer mused to herself as she continued to ponder on her friend and fellow worker ant Tenspeed. She knew that obedience to the Queen and securing her comfort and satisfaction and privacy were the natural way of things. At times, indeed, there was some sacrifice and discomfort involved. But the survival of the colony itself hinged greatly on Mother. They could in no wise survive without her.

"Besides, how would we know what to do every day," Gazer whispered to herself, "without the instructions the Queen sent out through her royal scent?" This was also the opinion of the majority of others.

This way of life had carried on in Entgora for many a season and many an ant generation, back far beyond antish remembrance.

3

the mishap

Once again mating season was upon Entgora, and Gazer knew it was so. She smelt the presence of winged males in the colony as she scampered along one of the tunnels to a work site she had been assigned to by one of the soldier ants. To her, males had a more pungent scent—almost like that of yellow fruits that the ants occasionally scavenged outside the hill—than that of her fellow worker females. A new Queen—or Princess—would secrete a scent into the air to attract the males, telling them the time was nigh. The males were always ready, willing, and able to render her their reproductive services.

A Princess could not mate with every male ant, so she would allow into her lair only the few who had the strongest odour. The stronger the reek, the stronger the male. And the stronger the male, the stronger the hope her offspring had of surviving and thriving in a hostile new world.

The males were typically smaller than even the worker ants, and they had wings. But, to Gazer and the other female workers and soldiers they looked strange and not fair in the least, especially with those long-flitting wings stretching far out from their bodies. They wondered why Queens young and old mated with them at all. It was likely a necessary evil to ensure the start of another colony, or so some thought.

As she moved swiftly to her task site, Gazer was glad she

was not a Queen ant, but just a lowly worker with a simple life and straightforward duties.

Along with a crew of thirty other workers, including her friends Buzzjaw and Shooter, she arrived at one of the outer walls that had been damaged from the last rainfall. It had thinned and needed to be thickened once again before another torrent of rain would utterly bring it to ruin.

The Pokers had brought in from the outside some twigs, as well as some stones and clumps of dirt that were to be rent apart into more manageable pieces and wedged into the damaged section of the wall. The Poker soldiers supervised the work and aided in some of the heavier tasks.

"In the name of the Queen! Take heed, little workers!" shouted the soldier ant in charge. "We've much work ahead of us this day. This wall must be mended. We soldiers will help you along with anything that's too trying for you workers." The soldier ant let out a little snickering chomp of her jaws. Some of the other soldiers also chuckled quietly. Soldiers, both Shouters and Pokers, were loyal to the Queen and clearly in command. Workers took comfort in the belief that they were more clever than all the soldiers and had more practical work experience, so these insults at their smallishness did not trouble them greatly. Gazer rehearsed in her mind the common worker rhyme that said as much.

A Poker and Shouter did set out one day
And stumbled across some fair food
The Poker did poke it
The Shouter decried it
And both were so terribly rude

A worker then came by to see all the fuss
Then munch-a-crunched up all the food
She walked off and said

"It's all in the head,
And thanks for the snack, it was good"

"Listen up now!" the soldier continued shouting, which brought Gazer's attention back to the present task. "The damage runs up high above the ground along this wall. And so, we need a few of you to scale the wall and do some repairs up there. You, you, and also you! Now to your work!"

One of those chosen was Gazer. But she gave it no mind. In fact, she gleefully accepted being called on to climb the wall, because she had always admired the winged beasties of prey she would sometimes fondly watch fly overhead.

And so they toiled.

The workers and soldiers bit all along the outside surface of the dirt chunks with their jaws. *Chomp, chomp, chomp!* The large gaping jaws of the huge soldier ant nearest her startled Gazer. She wondered if the strength of manifold antish jaws was equal to that of the long-nosed and long-tongued Outside Beast that was said to suck ants up at will on one of its horrid raids. She knew that unaided, she was no match in size or strength to either an Outside Beast or a soldier, even though she could hoist many times her own weight. She was glad that at least the soldiers were allied to her.

Gazer heard the joyful buzzing sound that Buzzjaw always made when chomping away. *Brrrzzz, brrrzzz, brrrzzz!* Buzzjaw was likely the strongest worker ant many had ever seen and, if fate had been any kinder, would have been born a soldier. Sometimes she privately hoped this were the case. And Shooter—who was so named because she sprayed acid quickly and aggressively whenever she sensed any kind of danger—was working away helping Buzzjaw. They always did things together.

The workers and Pokers chomped on their own bits of dirt until the soldiers could feel the dirt balls breaking apart slightly. Then the workers thrust their heads into the grooves and chipped at the centre as two soldiers each lay hold of the dirt ball halves and jerked hard, until it was rent in two. The soldier ants then went on to the next large dirt ball that was to be broken apart.

Gazer picked up the first smaller bit and plugged it into a hole in the wall that was near the ground. She then tried hoisting the next dirt bit, which was quite a bit heavier, and had some trouble. A soldier ant rushed over and helped raise the bolus onto Gazer's back.

"In the name of the Queen! Come now, little worker, get a move on," cried the Poker. Gazer was unsure if the soldier was trying to boost her confidence or fell it.

This next dirt ball had to be taken a little higher up along the wall to plug another hole. Thus, Gazer began to scale the wall slowly with her heavy load.

The surface was dampish from the rain that had caused the damage. The wall was difficult to climb and was more and more slippery the higher she went. Yet, Gazer pushed on.

She arrived at her target and steadied herself. As she began to push the dirt ball into the damaged area, her front legs gave way, and she slipped off the wall!

"Aaa-eeee-aaa-eeee!" screamed Gazer, as she fell headlong to the ground.

Her head slammed against the dirt floor. *Thump!* The rest of her body then hit the ground, sending waves of fiery pain through each of her six legs. The large dirt ball then came crashing down on her head, twisting her left antenna back and snapping it off!

She was stunned and lay still for some time, while a few soldier ants came over to inspect the scene. Buzzjaw and Shooter halted their labour to see what had happened to their friend, but were ordered back to work. As one of the soldiers helped Gazer find her legs, the other patted Gazer's body with her antennae, asking questions, assessing injuries, and discerning if Gazer was in any state to resume work. The soldier ants took notice that this worker had lost an antenna. She could not carry on with her duties that day.

"In the name of the Queen! You are done for the day, little worker! You best be getting home for some rest!" chirped the soldier, as she applied some saliva to the gash on Gazer's head where her left antenna was once proudly anchored.

Forlorn and with throbbing head, with Buzzjaw and Shooter watching, Gazer hobbled alone through one of the dark tunnels that would lead her back to her cramped group cell to rest and heal.

4

the mazework

Gazer turned left. Then right, following a long corridor for some time. Then up a steep slope. This route home was not a new one, but it seemed unfamiliar. Perhaps it was her headache. Perhaps it was the blurrish vision that would come and go in waves. Maybe it was the pain she still felt in her gut. She was tired too. More likely, it was the fact that she just lost her left antenna, which helped her with navigation, smell, and balance. In any case, she ascribed the unfamiliar path home to one of these symptoms.

Gazer stopped. Fighting off the pain, she lifted her head and with some difficulty wiggled her one remaining antenna. Where was she? She knew she was lost, but perchance she could pick up a well-known scent or breeze that would lead her back to the right pathway. Now and again, an ant would lose its way while outside on a food forage if it could not pick up any liquid trail left along the ground by another ant to get back home. During her days, Gazer had been through many parts of the maze-like grid that permeated the anthill while on various work duties. But this was new territory. She must have stumbled into an unfinished district of the hill.

Not a good way to come to my end of days, she thought. It sounded like something she had said before during a routine food foray on the outside. She was reminded of the strange breeze she felt that day. And of the odd fear that surged through her at the thought of being sucked up by an Outside Beast. What a commonplace way to come to her end. She remembered she was alone then. And she also found herself alone now.

Gazer started to move again, but more rapidly, hoping to find her way back to the main passageways that could lead her to her own cozy little cell. The choice of which tunnels to take, whether to turn left or right, now mattered not since she truly was lost.

She rushed along into a very wide and long corridor. The walls of this tunnel were unusually smooth, much more so than any she had seen before. They were smoother than she herself could make. She doubted whether she could even scale these walls and would likely just slide down. And the shape of the corridor was circular. It had been crafted with great skill.

As she reached the end of the tunnel, a brightness hit her eyes and a warmth washed over her body. She slowed and then came to a full stop, hitting a wall of her own fear. Her ever-present survival instinct kept her from lunging forward any further into possible peril. But a certain unfamiliar feeling grew that felled the wall.

Curiosity pushed her onward.

She hugged her body against the wall of the tunnel. And stepped forward, patiently, quietly, one leg after the other, feeling each patch of ground under her feet, almost as if approaching an unwary prey.

As she came to the mouth of the tunnel, Gazer stopped and shrank back. She was now staring into the largest and most beautiful cell she had ever seen in all of her days. It was perfectly round and was equally as wide as it was high. And the surfaces were smoother than even the carefully crafted tunnels leading to this secret place.

And it was bright. The light—which came from above through a hole in the ceiling—dispersed in rainbow colours like a waterfall through the entire cell as it poured through the end of the hole, whose edges were decorated with shiny, clear, many-coloured stones. The colours bathed her eyes and, for an instant, she forgot about the pain in her head and body and that she had lost an antenna. Or even that she was lost.

At the far end of the chamber, she spied several large stores of sundry foods. A feast ready to be consumed. Some of the food she recognized, as it was part of the usual worker ant diet. But some she had never seen before and had surely never tasted. It all looked tasty, and there was an abundance of it. She would have stepped closer and sampled some had she not already had her ration for the day. She was not one to take food away from fellow ants, who toiled just as hard as she. This sort of hording was frowned upon. And she cared not to do such an evilish thing.

She saw a great glistening pool of clear water at the wall opposite her. There were small bits of flower petals of many colours floating on the surface of the pool. She imagined not what they might be for. They seemed to serve no practical purpose.

On the ground in the centre of this cell lay a large green leaf that was newly arrived from the outside. Gazer knew it to be fresh from the scent in the air and from the richness of its deep green. More food? A contrivance to be used for a repair project of some importance? She did not know.

She thought that this was perhaps a meeting chamber or resting cell for a large group of Poker soldier ants. Or, perhaps this was a new food storage chamber that had been constructed. It could even be sanctuary for many an ant in the event of a raid from the mythical and dreaded Outside Beast.

Then something else dawned on Gazer. The cell was empty. No other ants were in sight, and this disturbed her. Much of the time ants were either in close quarters resting or would not be too far off from the crowd, even when performing solitary repair or food duties assigned by the soldier ants.

With her one remaining antenna moving round in a circular fashion, she was hit by a stench that was as overpowering as it was unwelcome. She staggered back a few more steps as the smell pushed her back. What was that scent? Why so pungent?

Out of the corner of her eye, she saw the movement of a shadow near the mouth of one of the other tunnels that led to this concealed chamber. She shrank back another step. And then she heard a sound. It grew louder, echoing through the mouth of the tunnel. Perhaps it was an Outside Beast come to raid the hill. Its hideous tongue was now sliding its way through this passageway in the hopes of slurping up a few ants as it slithered along.

Gazer dared not stir or make any kind of sound. She lowered herself against the ground, hoping the darkness of the tunnel would cover her in safety. She even stopped caressing the air with her antenna. A figure finally emerged into the chamber. Gazer's body was flooded by a sense of relief. It was no beastly tongue. It was a large, youthful, beautiful, female ant. And Gazer was shocked. She had never seen such a thing before—this female had wings! She was neither a worker nor a soldier.

Who was she then?

5

the ritual

The winged female ant pranced into the chamber. She was larger than even the average soldier ant and had a confident look about her. And her face was decorated with a white coating. She walked smoothly and almost hovered across the floor like the flower petals floating overtop the pool of water. And her wings bounced softly against her back with each step.

She dipped her head down and slurped on the water for such a long time that Gazer thought that she might have to save this winged creature from drowning. Eventually the ant came up for air.

Then the ant walked over to the food pile and picked up a piece of fruit, squeezed its juices down her throat using her sideways jaws, and then spewed the solid bit against the ground. She ate and ate and ate some more with a kind of grotesque gurgling sound. Gorging herself in fact. Eating many times what the average worker would consume over the course of an entire day.

Stretching out her wings and limbs and letting out a long and drawn out satisfied squeal, she plopped down onto the green leaf in the centre of the chamber and fell fast asleep.

This was neither a resting place nor a feeding station for a cadre of soldiers. Nor was it a haven in case of an Outside Beast attack.

It was the private chamber of this ant.

Gazer glared at the slumbering figure. She had never seen in all her days any ant drink and eat so much. She had never seen such luxurious private living quarters. Ants worked hard. They were practical. They rationed their food. And shared with one another. And they did things together in groups. Teamwork was the antish way of life. That was how the colony survived. She was confused and furious. But what was this? Who was this greedy little thing?

"My Princess," said a hollow voice echoing through one of the other corridors, rousing the sleeping ant. "My Princess, the time for the Ritual has come."

"Yes, yes, I'm prepared. Escort them in," cooed the Princess as she lifted her head up from her deep green bed.

In walked three winged male ants, accompanied by an equal number of Shouter soldiers—distinguished from Poker soldiers by their white painted faces—who were either protecting the males or making sure there was no escape. Gazer could not decide which. Her body remained fixed against the hard ground of the tunnel.

"Bring them closer so I can inspect them," commanded the Princess. The Shouters escorted the males a few steps closer. The Princess rose from her bed and studied each male's features as she circled round them and teasingly caressed their small frames with her wings.

"Yes, yes. Fine specimens. They will do very nicely. Very nicely indeed. They will be fine fathers for my newborns. Now, you do know that you'll be expelled from Entgora and perish after this is done within a few days, somewhere on the outside of the hill, by yourselves, all alone, don't you? Then I shall fly away in a few days, leaving this colony to give birth to my own somewhere far off."

The males wiggled their antennae without a word, acknowledging that they understood, but they were afraid.

"Alas, this is the order of things, after all, is it not?" the Princess asked, as she continued to circle the cowering trio. "My kind and I, after all, are vital to the survival of antish civilization. Yet you yourselves serve no other purpose but as tools to this greater end. I am sure you shan't take it personally. You are fulfilling your fit function and I mine," the Princess said in a conniving yet reassuring tone so persuasive that she nearly convinced Gazer. "Alas, I am conversing with mere fools, mere peons! It is time! Release the males!"

As the Shouters stepped back and huddled together, the males stood staring at the Princess. She stepped forward and began tensing her body and squeezing her belly against the ground repeatedly, sending out a scent so strong that Gazer almost fainted. The males became visibly enticed as they absorbed the aroma of the Royal One. Despite their overpowering yearning to mate, they were paralyzed with fear and dared not approach the Princess.

"Who will be the first to mate with me?" the Princess demanded. Seeing the hesitation of the males, she became enraged and bellowed, "Come closer, you imbeciles! Bashfulness is unwelcome here! Do your duty!" clucked the Princess.

The males stepped forward, and the four began their group mating frenzy.

The chirping and fluttering wing sounds pounded against Gazer's mind. She was aghast at the sights and sounds and smells. She could not abide them any longer and turned to run, but fell against the ground, twisting some of her legs. The pain was great, and she was unable to flee. She turned her head and tried to bury it between her body and the ground, attempting at least to conceal the hideous vision. Yet, as the moments passed, her curiosity and amazement grew. Although she knew witnessing this event was outlawed, Gazer could not conceal her high-pitched chirps of both dismay and enchantment, which became synchronized with the rhythm of the Ritual. She was cheeping more loudly than she had realized.

"Aaa-eee! What is this?" the Princess screamed, putting a halt to the mating ritual and motioning in the direction of Gazer's chirping sound. "What is that noise? Some wretched little thing lurks there in the shadows! There! There! Arrest that miserable ant!"

The Shouters pounced on Gazer, who was too weak and in pain to attempt an escape down the corridor. They dragged her into the chamber and dashed her to the ground at the feet of the Princess.

"Do you dare disturb the Ritual, you filthy little worker?" demanded the Princess.

Gazer was stunned and could only stammer, "My apologies, my liege. I was lost and…"

"Silence! It matters not!" roared the Princess. "You shall be justly dealt with later! Take her into detention. Let the Ritual continue!"

And as Gazer was dragged away by two Shouters through one of the long tunnels, she could hear the mating frenzy echoing after her mockingly.

6

the dream

Gazer and her escorts turned down a long corridor with low ceilings, passing prison cell after prison cell occupied mostly by workers but also a few soldiers. Each cell was guarded by two Pokers. There were hundreds of prisoners. Who knew the wretchedness of their crimes? Some sort of un-antlike thoughts and un-antlike behaviour. As she passed each one, Gazer guessed at their crimes from their features and body language. Laziness? Overeating? Disobedience? Originality?

Gazer finally arrived at her destination and was thrust into a cell by the soldiers. It was a dank little chamber, barely enough to stretch out in, and was more suitable in size for males than workers. Certainly, a soldier would fit inside only with some effort.

One Shouter and two Pokers arrived soon after. The Shouter was more seasoned and sombre than most others and even in hatchlinghood was thought by her elders to be overly aloof, never relishing to play with the others of her brood. And she never cared to use or be called by her given name, Gloomelda, but preferred her official title. She stepped forward almost politely, and in an unemotional manner explained to Gazer her legal condition.

"In the name of the Queen! I am the Royal Counsel, and I act as the Chief Legal Counsellor to Mother and as the Grand

Examiner of Entgora. I have come to inform you that you are officially charged with desecrating the mating Ritual of a Princess. As such, you will be detained here until you undergo inquiry tomorrow morning, at which time you will be formally tried, your sentence will be pronounced, and it will then be carried out. You will be provided with some water and fruit nectar at regular feeding cycles until such time. All else will be made clear on the morrow. Good day to you." And with that, the Counsel turned and whisked herself away, leaving Gazer in the company of her two guards.

Gazer slumped back down into her cell and pondered the day. Did ever an ant have such a day? First, a traumatic accident at work that left her with only one antenna. Then losing her way. Then discovering the most beautiful chamber she had ever laid eyes on. Then that beastly little Princess. As Gazer recalled the features of her face, she became more and more furious, wishing that the Outside Beast would someday slurp up the Princess. How could an ant behave in that way? Greedy. Barbarous. Arrogant. Maybe it should be the Princess enduring the shame of this trial instead. Yet, in Gazer's mind, bewilderment and fascination and logic all vied for victory over the breeding ritual she had witnessed. Perhaps the order of things was good and needful for the survival of the colony.

Gazer was exhausted. She was too downcast to allow her thoughts to linger there any longer. It was late. And she determined to get some sleep before the trial the next day.

As she drifted off, she fell into a dream.

She found herself completely alone. Far from her anthill. Far from any ants or other creatures. Far from flowers, trees, fruit, and rocks. Far from all that was familiar. She was standing on flat ground somewhere in a desert. She looked around and saw no footprints. And so she could not return from whence she came. The light was high in its midday place. And the sky was clear blue. Bluer than she had ever seen. Otherwise, there was nothing else in sight. She felt a soft breeze blow against her face. An unusual type of wind. Not cold or hot. It was steady and refreshing. It began to blow up some of the desert dust. It was a kind wind, but also untamed.

Far off in the distance, she saw a smallish black speck hovering above the ground. It grew larger and larger, very slowly but very steadily. And it was moving towards her. She watched it for the longest time. Still, she was unable to make out what it was because it was so far off. As the object moved closer to her, Gazer recognized the familiar scurrying movements. Joy filled her body. It was another ant! Good news! Company! Now she could perchance discover how to depart this desert and return home to her anthill. And with this, Gazer so much desired to walk, then trot, then run towards the other ant. Yet, she could not move. She was paralyzed. Somehow, she knew she had to wait for the other ant to arrive.

As the ant approached, Gazer began to make out her features. No wings. A female. Pale white, unlike her own black colour. About the same size as Gazer, and so a fellow worker ant to be sure. But there was something different and yet familiar about this creature. She had never seen this ant before and yet felt close to her, as if she had known her all her days. As the other ant arrived to where Gazer stood, they were face-to-face, and their eyes locked. Gazer studied the ant for a few moments.

"Peace to you, Gazer," the pale ant offered in a soothing way.

"Peace to you too, fellow ant," replied Gazer gladly. "How do you know my name? Which way back to Entgora? I'm glad you've come because I didn't know if…"

"Peace!" commanded the pale ant. Gazer quieted herself, deciding to listen rather than blurt. "I have come from far off," the ant continued. "I have come to meet with you alone! For the days are evil, and who knows whose antennae are twitching at this very moment? I bring with me tidings of what was, what is, and what is yet to be. I know that you will not understand. You are not meant to understand."

"What must I do then? How will I know what to do with what you tell me?" asked Gazer.

"Your task is to learn the song I will sing for you and find your place in it and help others do the same. But, be forewarned, few will find their place, for many will be called but few will enter in. Give heed now, for I will sing it only once." The ant then lifted her head, stretched back her antennae, inhaled deeply, and sang a song that began as a wispy limerick and ended as a dreadful dirge.

From ancient days a seed was sown
That filled Pangaea's womb
Which birthed new life that trod the earth
From new hatched egg to tomb

But those of greed and haughtiness
Do crown their heads with pow'r

And stomp their feet on endless march
Until their judgment hour

So war shall come from tribes far off
Like wind sweeps west to east
A flow'r that's plucked up by its roots
Shall in new soil find peace

The order soon will sleep in death
Its corpse shall stink and spoil
The head and tail will change their place
Till ev'ry ant be royal

Then beastly horde will rise and stand
And tread both great and small
The meek shall then inherit earth
And flee the coming fall

Gazer absorbed the words and let the feeling of the song sink into her before she dared speak. "Is this good news or bad news? I cannot tell. Is this for me alone? Am I to teach others the song? How can I find my place in it, if I cannot grasp its meaning? You must help me to uncover its secrets."

The pale white ant stared for some time at Gazer without a word. Then she finally spoke. "Many from ages past have desired to know these things, but it has been granted to you and those of your time. You will know what to do when the moment comes. Fear not. Now your task is your own!"

With this, the ant turned away from Gazer and traced her footsteps back along the path by which she came.

"Sister ant, what is your name? You did not tell me your name!" Gazer shouted after the ant, yet to no avail. The pale white ant was deaf to Gazer's pleas. She walked away slowly, until she was seen no more.

7

the trial

"In the name of the Queen! The dawn has come. Wake up little worker," called out one of the Pokers. Gazer was still drowsy from sleep, but had vivid images swirling about in her mind of a desert and a pale white ant. And she was humming the melody to a strange song. She gradually realized she was being held in a prison cell. And that there was a trial this morning. Her trial. Last night was a dream, after all.

Gazer could hear echoes down the corridor of clickity-clacking jaws and shuffling feet all along the line of prison cells. Pokers were bringing small bits of fruit to the prisoners, who were then squeezing out the juice and returning the leftovers for disposal. There were minor verbal skirmishes between some prisoners and their guards over cell cleanliness and food quality. This was morningmeal.

Finishing her food, Gazer gave the dry leftover fruit to the soldier and lay hold of her guard's leg to steal her attention. "When will it be? When am I scheduled for trial?" Gazer asked.

"In the name of the Queen! The Royal Counsel will make her rounds as usual today. She will come for you soon." The soldier then turned away and, along with a group of others, went along from cell to cell to collect the morningmeal refuse and transport it outside the hill. But most of the guards remained on duty.

Gazer settled down for the wait. Her thought turned to the dream of the night before. It was easy to bring to the surface. It was still fresh. And its strength was burned into her. She turned the images over and over in her mind like she would turn food around with her antennae and forelegs, examining each side closely, looking for any distinct features before clamping on with her sideways jaws. A desert. A pale white ant. A song of wars, flowers, corpses, and beasts. The more she explored, the more murky it became. A dream perhaps brought on by the stresses of the day and the fear of trial. And the attempts of a ravaged mind to soothe and shield itself.

Her long trance was broken by the parting of the guards. The prison Counsel stepped between them and hovered at Gazer's cell entrance.

"In the name of the Queen! Worker ant, your trial is at hand," the Counsel decreed. "Soldiers! You will escort this little worker ant and follow me to the Hall of Reckoning!"

Gazer exited her cell into the corridor, having one soldier ant ahead and one behind her, with the Counsel leading the procession. As the foursome trotted past the long row of prison cells, Gazer could hear calls of encouragement like "Pity! Pity!" and "May the Great Ant be with you!" from some of the inmates. Others called out to the Counsel that they were innocent and belonged not in this dungeon. That they should be set free. Or vowed they should never do such an evil deed again. Most ants, however, clickity-clacked their jaws together in unison repeatedly, which was the usual fashion in which workers saluted one another. All these distractions fell to the ground or ricocheted from the walls. Yet, the Counsel gave no heed to the machinations of these lawbreakers.

The Counsel's convoy approached a guard of four Shouter soldiers standing in front of a large entranceway. Each pair of soldiers sidestepped in mirror fashion on sight of the Counsel to allow her and the small parade that followed to pass. "I reckon this must be the Hall of Reckoning," Gazer smirked to herself.

As they entered the massive round chamber, Gazer was beset by the chatter made by the throng of ants that lined the walls in what appeared to be two areas sectioned off for spectators, one for workers and one for Pokers. She had no reason to have been there before and recalled hearing only rumours of two other public trials in her lifetime, neither of which she attended. Trials in the colony were almost always clandestine events, and the one on trial was never laid eyes on again. Gazer's trial, however, was to be a public spectacle, which was sometimes done to fasten fear onto the masses and wreathe in them greater obedience to the Queen. She felt as lonesome as the one antenna still perched on top of her head. Yet, her heart leapt as she saw some familiar faces in the worker section. There they were: Tenspeed, Shooter, and Buzzjaw.

"Gazer! Gazer! May the Great Ant be with you!" called out Tenspeed. Her friends waved their antennae at Gazer, and she returned the greeting.

As she walked through the parted crowd of ants, Gazer's eyes met with each pair of eyes belonging to ant faces engraved all along the walls of the Hall. These were images of generations of past Queens of Entgora, each with faces smeared decoratively with white pigment. She did not recognize any of them and counted their number only with some effort. By each image were symbols from the High Entgoran language of olden times with which Gazer and most other ants were unfamiliar. She finally arrived at a raised mound of dirt in the middle of the room. It was here that she was to take her stand. It was one of a triad of mounds. The soldier escort now left Gazer, while the Counsel took a few steps forward to stand in the centre between the mounds.

Gazer twitched and brooded at the sight of the approaching Princess. Her steps were proud and deliberate. She was greeted in recognition by some of the Pokers by low clickity-clacky sounds. She also took her stand on one of the three dirt mounds and deigned not to look at Gazer, who glanced over a few times at the young royal.

The Counsel turned to the chattering mass of ants and called for their attention. "In the name of the Queen!"

"In the name of the Queen!" the section of soldier spectators shouted back. The worker section clickity-clacked its jaws.

"In the name of the Queen! All raise your antennae for Her Royal Majesty Queen Entvladarka," the Counsel shouted proudly, "the High Protectress and Lawgiver of Entgora, the Mother of all Entgoran Ants, and the Direct Descendant and Successor of the Great Ant!"

The Pokers saluted with antennae raised and with loud chirping noises, each competing with each other as to who could stretch out their antennae higher in honour of their sovereign. It was a show of ant prowess. Perhaps they might receive notice for their feisty expressions of loyalty to the Queen and be promoted to the admired elite circle of Shouter ants.

The Queen of Entgora walked in from a side chamber accompanied by a bodyguard of three white-faced Shouter ants and took her position on the third dirt mound, facing both the Princess and Gazer. The Shouters remained stationed behind the Queen, watching the crowds for disorderly conduct. This was the first time that many Pokers, workers, and certainly Gazer herself had ever seen the Queen face-to-face. She was roundish and large in stature—perhaps two or three times the size of a Shouter ant, with perhaps the exception of the Princess—and likely so big because she still retained a good deal of male sperm from previous mating rituals. She was also wingless, which surprised Gazer because the Princess, being a future Queen of her own colony, was still possessed of her wings. And her face was decorated with a white hue after the fashion of the Shouters and the Princess. Some of the tooth-like jaggedness of the Queen's jaws had been smoothed from much daily use over her lengthy life and from wartime injuries. The Queen was plainly also the oldest by many seasons than any other ant in the colony. Gazer detected a look of experience, wisdom, and perhaps even kindness in the royal face.

"My dear children," began the Queen, motioning to those gathered, "your Mother greets you! May the peace and blessings of Entgora, the unbroken chain of Entgoran Queens, and the Great Ant be upon you all. Today we are gathered here in this great Hall of Reckoning to deal with a serious charge: that of desecrating the sacred mating Ritual. For those of you for whom it is the first time to observe these public reckonings, I

34

will explain the nature of the proceedings. I am the final Reckoner concerning charges and sentencing. Our illustrious Grand Examiner and Royal Counsel will act in her usual role as Accuser. Those accused do not have access to a counsellor but must defend themselves, because it is my law that states that an ant is guilty until proven innocent. One of the two ants standing before you will come to her end of days on the morrow. That is a certainty. For it is also my law that hatred must not exist between Entgoran ants. And for as long as both of these ants live, their hatred shall exist. To destroy this hatred, one of these ants must also be destroyed. It is only my act of pity that allows one of them to continue in this life. At the end of today's trial, therefore, I will decide which ant must die, for it is my law that states that the Queen decides such things. Royal Counsel, please proceed."

"In the name of the Queen!" began the Counsel. "Mother, before you stands this Princess, who is accusing this little worker of disturbing and endangering the success of her Ritual. Princess, please state your name and explain to Mother the events of the day in question."

The Princess responded in carefully measured tones. "Dear Mother, respected Counsel, and soldiers, greetings to you. My name is Princess Entrata, and Mother gave birth to me many days ago and judged it right that I would one day become a Queen and give birth to my own colony of ants upon my departure from Entgora. As you know, our Mother gives birth to thousands upon thousands of ants over many seasons. This ensures that our great colony of Entgora survives and thrives from generation to generation and that new colonies are birthed throughout the entire land of Pangaea. This is the order from ancient days, from times long forgotten. It has been my good fortune to have been born a Princess, charged with the sacred duty of beginning such a colony. As part of my service to Mother, I began the mating Ritual with three male ants in my private chambers a few days ago."

The Princess paused and began to sway side to side—with her wings rising slightly off her back—and to chirp softly as if she had just been wounded.

"In the name of the Queen! Please Princess, continue," consoled the Counsel.

"As I was in the midst of the Ritual, I heard a chirping sound behind me that grew louder and louder. I had to stop. And when I turned around, it was that, that..." The Princess turned and pointed at Gazer with both of her antennae and screamed, "That one-antennad little worker ant interrupted the Ritual and attempted to prevent its completion!"

At this, Gazer shrivelled into herself and clicked and chirped softly. The entire Reckoning chamber too exploded into loud chirp-chorps and clickity-clacks and cries of "Treason! Treason!" Both soldiers and workers were shocked at what they heard. How could someone dare endanger the life of future generations of ants and colonies? Gazer's friends Tenspeed, Shooter, and Buzzjaw looked at each other, astonished but unsure of whether to believe it. They had heard the rumours that Gazer was arrested—and so came to the Reckoning—but they assumed it was for laziness at having left the work site a few days ago after her fall from the wall. But this? Treason? It was too horrible to bear!

"Clickity-clack! Clickity-clack! Clickity-clack!" the Queen interrupted loudly. "Children, children, quiet in the Hall of Reckoning! Quiet!" The roar of the ants quickly subsided into murmurs. "Royal Counsel, please continue!"

"In the name of the Queen! Thank you, Mother. And thank you, Princess Entrata, for your bravery in reliving for us such a horrendous experience. Please now, tell us how your ordeal, your horrible ordeal, reached its end."

The Princess inhaled deeply and carried on. "Thanks be to the Great Ant, for I had with me three Royal Soldiers who rescued me and protected me from this fiendish little worker ant's plot!"

"In the name of the Queen! Thank the Great Ant indeed! As you can see, dear Mother and beloved guests," the Counsel continued, "this case is as clear as the Waters of Darktree."

Some soft chirps of approval and agreement were heard from the spectators in the crowd.

"In the name of the Queen!" the Counsel continued. "Mother, the Princess ceases the formal accusation. May I have permission to proceed to an examination of the accused?" The Queen nodded in approval.

The Counsel turned to Gazer and assaulted her with questions. "In the name of the Queen and in the sight of the Great Ant, little worker, did you not see the Princess engaged in the Ritual without her knowledge? Were you not at her private chambers without permission? Did you not, in fact, come to the Princess's chambers to stop the Ritual and, therefore, to stop the formation of a new Entgoran ant colony? And does your one antenna not give you away? Do you not belong to some villainous faction bent on the destruction of our civilization? Are you not, perhaps, a spy working for the dreaded warrior ants of Entmerika, also known as—dare I utter the words—the Blue Grey Hordes?"

"No, this is not true! It was all a mere mishap. I lost my antenna at one of the assigned work sites and then lost my way," Gazer said firmly as she steadied herself on her dirt mound. But to no avail. Her words were drowned out by the wave of fear-filled chirps and cheeps and whistles and whimpers and clicks and clacks from the great swarm of ants in the hall. Mayhem! Even the Queen was swaying side-to-side and chirping loudly. The only one not showing any signs of fear was the Royal Counsel, who merely observed the grand scene and stood smugly in the power of her own oratory.

The noise slowly subsided. Gazer looked over at her friend

Tenspeed and her two companions and slowly shook her head, pleading with her eyes that the accusations were untrue. They returned her gaze and understood. Or so she hoped. The Queen motioned with her antennae and two forelegs for complete silence in the hall. The din was quelled.

"My children," the Queen began, "the truth to me is as visible as the Stone of Greenwood. We have here a case of, dare I say it, treason! Treason against the Queen! Treason against Entgora! Treason against all Entgoran ants! I thank the Princess Entrata for being so brave in her testimony. And for the learned Royal Counsel's efforts in the case before us. Worker ant called Gazer, I trust that you appreciate your situation. I find you guilty of the charge of treason! Your name will be forbidden from being spoken by the jaws of Entgoran antkind. You are to be punished as were heretics and rabble-rousers and evildoers and dreamers of bygone days, as recorded in the sacred Chronicles of Entgora. You are hereby sentenced to death by drowning—the most shameful death an ant can endure—to pay for your crime. The sentence will be carried out on the morrow at lightrise. Do you have any last words for those gathered here today in the Hall of Reckoning?"

"Dear Mother," replied Gazer, "I am no traitor. The case the Counsel presented was not fully the truth, but only a twisted version of it. Remember the old antish proverb that says, 'An ant that shares her food loves others as herself. An ant that hides her food loves only herself. But an ant that lets her food spoil before it's eaten by anyone, has forgotten what food is for.' "

Some clicks and clacks of agreement were heard echoing through the Hall.

Gazer continued. "My Queen, I cherish Entgora. I was born an Entgoran and will die one at my end of days. But, if this is your final reckoning, dear Mother, then, if I may say so humbly, I will be honoured to die the same death as that of the

Great Ant."

"In the name of the Queen! Peace! Silence!" erupted the Counsel angrily as she leapt forward a few steps, violently thumping Gazer on the head with her forelegs and sending her crashing to the ground. *Thud!*

The crowds gasped at the display, some in delight and some in fear.

"Do not presume to compare yourself to the Great Ant!" the Counsel added, as she hovered over Gazer.

As Gazer raised herself slowly from the ground without a word and avoiding eye contact with the Counsel, the Queen wondered at how a little worker ant could be at the same time so sincere and insolent, brave and dim-witted, admirable and pitiable.

"My children, the matter is concluded," interrupted the Queen. "Let us now keep silence and implore the Great Ant in thanks to conclude the Reckoning."

The hall became so silent a leaf petal dropping to the ground could be heard.

The Queen called upon her hearer, with antennae and forelegs raised. "O Great Ant! Give heed to the words of our entreaties. We thank thee for being the Shield of Entgora, protecting our righteousness from the wicked ways of our enemies. We thank thee for being the Revealer of Truth, showing it to those who are enlightened and keeping it hidden from fools. We thank thee for being the Fount of Wisdom, eternally bestowing understanding on the Queen so that her righteous laws and judgment might be fulfilled. We thank thee for being the Stone of Entgora, giving us firm courage to carry out your justice, sparing not the ant, lest the colony be spoiled. May it be so."

The Queen then motioned to a pair of Royal Soldiers. "Remove the walking dead from the hall and back to her holding cell to await our justice." She left her mound and exited the hall into the side chamber she first emerged from with her own escort of Shouters.

The Princess and Counsel conferred together as they watched Gazer surrounded by two Shouters and the original two Pokers that brought her to the hall.

Gazer became downcast as the murmur of chirps and clicks in the hall grew.

"Despair not!" Tenspeed called out, as Gazer was escorted through the hall by soldiers, past the engravings on the wall, through the exit hole, and back into the labyrinth of dark passageways.

8

the blue grey hordes

It was the middle of the night, long after lightfall. Gazer lay fast asleep in her cell after the nightmare of the trial. The pair of guards along the prison corridor positioned outside each of the many cells took turns sleeping and dreaming. But, for Gazer this time, no dreams would come to comfort her mind. Even asleep she was facing the reality of being charged with treason and of her upcoming doom. Still, she felt serene crammed deep in her cell, almost like a butterfly in her cocoon awaiting metamorphosis and flight.

Then it began. *Harrrooom! Harrrooom! Harrrooom!* A low rumbling vibration of the ground. It grew louder, and it was enough to awaken some of the ants in Entgora from their sleep, including Queen Entvladarka.

Still drowsy and draggy from sleep in her private chamber—the Womb—deep in the hill, the Queen hoisted the weight of her large body with some difficulty, raised her antennae, and began sniffing the stale air. Nothing. The noise was likely not coming from outside her cell or from anywhere inside Entgora. She had been High Protectress of the colony for many a season and had fought during the First War of the West. And she knew there were few things that could make such a sound, but she had to be sure before alarming her citizens, many of whom were young and had as yet not gained much life experience.

"Royal Guards! Come here quickly," she called out. While still in the midst of her shouts, two white-faced Shouters charged with protecting her during her slumber came hurdling over one another into her room.

"In the name of the Queen! Mother, what has happened? What is the matter?"

"Shush! Quiet! Listen! Do you hear that sound?" The Queen paused to let the Shouters give heed to the noise. Their antennae circled slowly as their heads swayed left to right. They could not hear anything and, without a word, looked at the Queen with the look of the unenlightened. They were deafer than other ants because of all the shouting and undue antenna waving they did day-in and day-out. The Queen knew this, but could not abide it well.

"Fools! True enough that many call you Shouters. Truer yet if they called the pair of you deaf and dumb too. Can you feel the vibration of the ground? Stand still, and feel it run up your legs." The soldiers stood motionless and studied the dirt beneath their feet.

"In the name of the Queen! Yes Mother, we can feel it too! What is it? Where is it coming from?"

"Good," the Queen said sourly, "remind me to give the pair of you royal commendations for bravery and intelligence! Ah, it's good to know I'm not just talking to myself! Now quickly, recruit two more Royal Soldiers with you and go outside the colony. Each one of you is to scout towards the Four Great Winds. Then report back to me. In the name of the Great Ant! Speed, you fools!"

The Shouters left the worried Queen and scurried to a massive chamber named the Hollow, the main Shouter sleeping cavern. Some of the soldiers were stirring from their sleep because of the vibrating earth, but most were still in their rest cycle. The Queen's envoys tapped a pair of others on the head forcefully, startling and awakening them, who were then told of Mother's orders. The foursome made haste to exit through the nearest holeway, all along the way hearing a growing number of ants stirring from their sleep because of the now audible noise, *Harrrooom! Harrrooom! Harrrooom!*

When they arrived outside, the senior Shouter gave orders. "In the name of the Queen! Soldiers, sweep your antennae over the entire range every five paces until you reach one hundred and twenty paces towards each of the Four Great Winds! When you complete your task, report back here!"

The soldiers began their appointed duty and moved swiftly to four sides of the hill. At the fifth step, they stopped to whirl their antennae around, scanning left, right, up, and down, sniffing the air for any foreign smells, sounds, or sights...all the while fighting to keep their minds off the quaking earth and on their present mission. They did the same at the tenth, fifteenth, twentieth, twenty-fifth, thirtieth, and thirty-fifth steps.

At the fortieth step, the Shouter moving towards the great west wind lurched to a stop. She knew before she even surveyed the air that a still distant, but quite unwelcome, presence and force was approaching her. She could feel the wind pushing against her face, and then just as quickly whipping past her. She locked her gaze onto a distant point that was bibbidy-bobbing up and down. Her heart beat faster and faster. Then she began scanning her antennae wildly. She could smell it. And then she saw it clearly. A swarm of ants a thousand bodies wide and half as long was marching shoulder-to-shoulder in lockstep towards her and towards her home, Entgora.

The Shouters rendezvoused at their starting point and reported what they had seen and heard to one another. They rushed back to the Queen to inform her of what they had discovered. But they were all of them unsure of its true meaning.

Their arrival interrupted the Queen's pacing and her pleas

to the Great Ant. "What news do the winds bring?" asked the Queen in a low voice.

"In the name of the Queen! Mother," began the senior Shouter, "three of the winds bring no tidings, and they are at peace. The winds of the east, north, and south are pure and clean. But the west wind is foul with the stench of foreign ants. Thousands upon thousands of them, marching as a single body toward us. Who are they, Mother? What do they seek?"

The Queen stepped back, swayed side-to-side as if in a trance, and spoke slowly. "My children, these are the warrior ants of Entmerika. The Blue Grey Hordes! Most of Entgora's ants, because you are young, have never faced this threat but only know of them from story and legend. They come at will and without warning to kill, destroy, and enslave. I faced them many seasons ago as a young Queen. Great were the losses. We are being invaded! Prepare for battle!" At hearing her own words, the Queen snapped out of her hypnotic state. With the small troop of four soldiers, she marched off to the Hollow to address the Shouters.

The Queen commanded in a loud voice, "Royal Soldiers! Royal Soldiers! Awake! Arise! Prepare for battle! Prepare to defend Entgora! The armies of the Blue Grey Hordes are advancing on us from the west! They strike like lightning! They come to steal our food, enslave our numbers, kill any ant that resists, and take away our most cherished value—order! Wake every ant in Entgora, and assemble them in battle formation on the west side of the hill! We must meet them in the open! We are a weak quarry for them if we remain inside the hill! Leave no ant in the colony! Take them out by force if need be! We need every twitching creature to give fight! Place the prisoners on the frontline, then behind them all the workers, then soldiers, then any males, and finally the Royal Soldiers at the rear to make a last stand, if it comes to that! Go you fools! Speed!"

The Queen sent a strong scent from the Womb and into the colony's airways. The call to war. Meanwhile, the Shouters galloped from level to level and cell to cell down each corridor crying, "In the name of the Queen! The Hordes are coming! The Hordes are coming!" stopping briefly only to answer questions and give commands.

Shouters also made their way to the prison level sounding the same alarm about the invasion.

"The Hordes? What hordes? Why is the Queen sounding the alarm?" Gazer and the other prisoners cheeped at the excited group of Shouters.

"In the name of the Queen! The Blue Grey Hordes of the West have launched an assault on Entgora! We must all fight to survive, including you prisoners! Under the authority of Mother, your crimes are now forgiven you, if you fight willingly and valiantly!"

Gazer and the others rushed towards the nearest exit holes, happy at the clemency that was bestowed on them by Mother, but terrified by the unknown Blue Grey Hordes. Most of them were too youngish and had never come face to face with this enemy. And it was usually only the soldier ants who defended against smaller groups of intruder ants and other insects.

A steady stream of ants continued to flow out of the anthill and formed a wide battle line on the west side. Gazer found herself side by side on the frontline with hundreds of other prisoners. Behind her, she saw a vast multitude of workers and Pokers, huddled together row on row. Far to the rear, she spied the gleaming white faces of the Shouters reflecting the newly rising morning light.

A large group of Shouters from the rear came hurdling forward overtop of the heads of the Entgoran ant army to join the vanguard, sent there by the Queen to give courage and leadership to the workers, who had all received four cycles of mandatory basic training in ant-to-ant combat, but were far less experienced. They positioned themselves at equal spaces along the frontline in between the others. Some one hundred and twenty thousand were assembling themselves hastily and noisily. Entgora now stood almost empty, except for elder ants caring for young hatchlings.

Gazer stood nervously near the front and could hear chirping and clicking noises and conversations here and there among the Entgorans in anticipation of the approaching foe. She wondered where her friends Tenspeed, Shooter, and Buzzjaw were. She surveyed her comrades and caught a glimpse of Tenspeed a few rows over and called out to her.

"Tenspeed! Tenspeed! Over here!"

"Gazer, Miss Gazer! Indeed, indeed, I was just pondering on you and quizzed myself about how you just might be after that trying trial and if you had any thoughts about the battle—it's upon us now, without a doubt, without a doubt—and whether you were scared and whether your antenna still hurts and if you'd seen Buzzjaw or Shooter and what they were doing and..."

"Since you asked Tenspeed," Gazer interrupted, "I'm standing firm, but barely at that. And I had a dream the other night in my holding cell. A strange dream, Tenspeed, one so strange that, to use your words, it was as odd as a stone without a flat spot to sit on. There was an ant and beasts and flowers. Even winds and corpses and hordes. If we survive this fight, I'll have to tell you about it. Perhaps we can scamper off now away from all this and talk about it? I think we shall not be missed." Then Gazer chirped humorously, "Besides, I'm not in the mood for a war today. But I hear the wages are good, and the food is ripe. And I've nothing else planned."

Tenspeed cheeped back in laughter, "Right you are, Miss Gazer, right you are indeed!"

"And, no, I do not know where Shooter and Buzzjaw are," said Gazer. "But I'll wager you they're probably together, standing shoulder to shoulder, as usual."

"Tenspeed, may the Great Ant be with you!"

"And so she shall be, to be sure, to be sure! And the same to you, Gazer. And now let's get to the fight straightaway like all good ants should. And may the best ant win!"

"In the name of the Queen! Ants arise!" cried a Shouter, who was standing but a few ants from Gazer. "Ants arise!" exclaimed the other Shouters, to quiet and steady their army. Entgora now stood ready for battle! They turned their gaze forward to the approaching unseen adversary, whose marching sounds grew louder. *Harrrooom, harrrooom, harrrooom!*

The enemy then came out from under its cloak of invisibility. A mass of ants began to emerge into full view. The Blue Grey Hordes indeed! Gazer saw their frontline clearly. On the one side, the ants were blue. At the opposite, they were grey. And the ants in the middle were a mixture of both colours, gradually transitioning from one to the other as her eye moved along the line, giving the appearance of a foamy water wave or some slithery creature. This was to the younger Entgorans a terrifying sight.

"In the name of the Queen! Ants advance!" the Shouters cried. The entire mass of Entgorans moved together, making their own marching sound underfoot as they ploughed across the dusty ground. *Kabooom, kabooom, kabooom!* The Shouters then began to chant an Entgoran marching song used in their soldiery training. The workers marched and listened, hoping to draw some courage from the words.

Entgora, Entgora, we see thee stand and rise
Entgora, Entgora, we will stand tall and fight
We meet the foe unwavering
We face the battle strong
We use our antish weapons
We fight to right all wrongs

We brandish our antennae
And smell our rival well
We wage our war with six strong legs
And sound our foe's death knell
Entgora, Entgora, we see thee stand and rise
Entgora, Entgora, we will stand tall and fight

The song was almost drowned out by the deafening noise of marching ants. *Harrrooom! Harrrooom! Kabooom! Kabooom!*

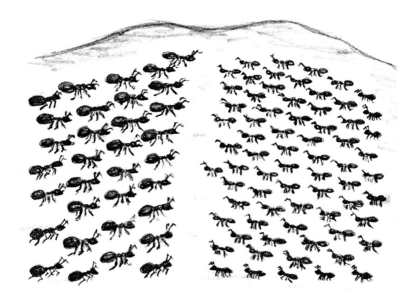

The two great armies of Entmerika and Entgora marched towards one another head on rapidly. Soon they were charging at full speed, and the sky echoed with loud clickity-clacks and high-pitched whistles and chirps. As the opposing frontlines met, their bodies dashed against one other, knocking many to the ground who were then trampled to death by friend and foe alike. Charging ants from both sides swept past their foes and tripped them with their extended forelegs, hoping that some would be trampled. Others locked antennae after crashing together and then wrestled with their forelegs and chomped at each other with their sideways jaws, shearing off limbs and antennae and even heads. Many ants from the rear of both armies ran overtop their densely packed marching comrades—using their backs and heads as stepping stones—and flung their own bodies into the opposing forces, toppling many.

Pairs of ants laid hold of larger stones and chunks of dirt, as well as dead and living ants, and launched them high into the air at the enemy army. Ants climbed on top of one another's backs three and four levels high in a line a dozen ants wide, creating moving walls that charged at the enemy and crashed down on them. Roaming bands of ants hunted the injured, falling on their adversary to bring about their speedy death.

From the Entgoran rear, a goodly number of winged male ants flew across the melee, carrying with them clumps of dirt and small stones, dropping them on top of the Entmerikans. *Plink!* Sometimes this pinned their enemies to the ground. At other times it crushed their heads and bodies, killing many instantly. The Entmerikans could use no such stratagem, as they were a wingless tribe of ants, including their Queen. The Entmerikan workers, however, had the advantage of being strongish and larger than the average Entgoran worker and were able to fight off several foes at the same time. Soon much of each army had washed into the other as wave after wave of ants flew at their foes, giving the appearance of a speckley sea of black and blue and grey and blood red.

Gazer found herself locked in an antenna and foreleg hold with a larger blue Entmerikan, who found it difficult to grapple with an ant possessed of only one antenna. This was the first time Gazer had seen this legendary enemy up close. She was as curious of this sight as she was fearful. To Gazer's great surprise, this creature looked similar to her own Entgorans. Antennae.

Six legs. Sideways jaws. Possibly a female, but that was not obvious. But definitely an ant. The foe was blue, rather than black. Somewhat larger than Gazer, perhaps the size of an Entgoran soldier. And hairier. The two eyes were much smaller and only single-chambered, unlike Gazer's many-chambered eyes. Gazer guessed this ant could not see well and was likely blind, from the unusual amount of its antenna waving and poking, much more so than any Entgoran.

The most uncomfortable difference was the horrible smell of this ant. One of the worst odours she had ever been assaulted by. "Even Entgoran males smelt better," Gazer chortled to herself.

These two foes chomped at each other and wrestled fiercely. Gazer pierced the enemy's left eye with her right antenna, permanently blinding it and inflicting fiery pain. The blue ant recoiled momentarily, but then leapt at Gazer with a ferocious screech, sending them both tumbling head over feet to the ground. Gazer was now on the bottom and now knew for a certainty indeed that this enemy was tough as stone and stronger than she, to the point that she feared her end had come. She desperately clawed and scratched and chomped at her assailant. Overtop her flew two Entgorans, ramming the blue creature off Gazer. It was Tenspeed and another ant Gazer did not know. Her rescuers had come. The three together then did slay their common enemy, leaving its body motionless on the ground, covered in dirt and blood.

Gazer sturdied herself. "Tenspeed! Thank you. And you too, fellow Entgoran! I thought I was at my end of days."

"To be sure, Miss Gazer! To be sure! Seein' that I have two eyes, I was pointin' my one bad eye at my enemies and I had the keen sense—thank the Great Ant—to keep the other good one firmly fixed on my friends. Oh, how rude I am indeed, indeed. Gazer, allow me to acquaint you with Digdirt," Tenspeed chirped.

"Much obliged, Digdirt. You show great skill with those jaws you wield." Gazer beamed.

"You are indeed welcome. There is not one thing I would leave undone for the sake of a fellow Entgoran, even that of giving my very life blood. But we best be getting back to the task at hand," concluded Digdirt, as she surveyed the battlefield with a look of might in her face.

"Quite right!" the other two agreed heartily.

As they trotted off, Gazer turned back for one last glance at the limp body of her slain foe, who looked noble in her peaceful, eternal sleep. What happened to these barbarians when they came to their end of days? Did they enter the bosom of the Great Ant like Entgorans? Even though she was glad about her rescue, she felt a tinge of regret at the downfall of this savage enemy. She was reminded of the old proverb:

From dust to ant and ant to dust
We in the Great One place our trust
From ant to dust and dust to sky
We see the Great One when we die

The trio plunged back into the fray of the main skirmishes on the field of battle. A short distance away, Shouters here and there were yelling orders as they ran among scattered groups of comrades, "In the name of the Queen! Ants of Entgora! Jaws of Death! Jaws of Death!" This cry called on the Entgorans to change their battle lines into the form of an enormous antlike sideways jaw that would pinch the enemy. The Entgoran workers retreated en masse, drawing the Enmerikans into giving them chase down the middle. The workers quickly closed ranks in the centre, turned, and charged back again towards the enemy with renewed vigour, while the Pokers and Shouters rushed to the far left and right, flanked their enemy and sped towards the middle, there to crush them. The

Entmerikans suffered great losses from the Entgoran assault. But the Entgoran workers died in greater numbers still, being caught themselves in the jaws they helped give life to.

Yet this was not to be the end of things that day. For in the distance, from the far left and far right, charged two battalions of Entmerikan ants, but none too numerous, perhaps only hundreds. They were each of them larger in stature than the first invasion force of workers that the Entgorans had managed to stalemate so far in the game.

These were the Entmerikan soldier ants. They rushed upon the bewildered masses but ravaged only a few Entgorans because of the thick defensive shield formed by the Pokers and Shouters.

Then came the Entmerikan shout, "The Ring! The Ring!" The Blue Grey Hordes, to the astonishment of all, suddenly formed a gigantic circular shield fifty ants deep that encompassed thousands of Entgorans, reversed course, and quickly disappeared from the battlefield back to the west, carrying off many injured and limping Entgorans.

Although a few Entgorans here and there made some attempts to penetrate the Entmerikan shield to rescue their ill-fated compatriots, it was to no avail. They had no cohesive strategy to deal with exotic events such as this and had only been trained in standard defensive shields, offensive assaults, and ant-to-ant combat, but not in rescue efforts which called for a different manner of warfare. The Entgorans, now alone on the west side of their anthill, looked on feebly. There was no mystery as to the fate of the prisoners of war. They were to be slaves in Entmerika.

The light was in its midday place, but none took notice. A call came from one of the Shouters, "In the name of the Queen! Collect the dead! Assist the wounded! Gather to the west!" And it was so. Thousands were dead, their bodies and body parts strewn across the field of blood, now mingling with the dirt to make a reddish brown mud. Chirps and whistles of grief were heard as workers and soldiers gathered their fallen comrades onto Entgora's southern refuse heap, which was commonly reserved for feces, food litter, and dead ants who died of oldishness. The wounded were carried or assisted to the western side of Entgora, where the entire colony was now gathered facing the hill. The Queen, in due course, came into view and perched herself on top of a large stone placed there by a troop of Shouters.

"My dear children!" the Queen began, as she waved her antennae and forelegs to draw the attention of the multitude. "My dear children! This day will live in our memories, from everlasting to everlasting. From this day to our end of days, we will all remember with great pride in our chests how we defeated and gave chase to the savage hordes that attacked us unprovoked. When you are old, you will retell the tale of this battle to young hatchlings, to whom you will be a living example of the virtues of Entgora and what it means to live an honourable life. They will know for a certainty that the righteous always triumph over the evildoer. And we will bring to our remembrance our cherished comrades who fell this day and the many who were wounded defending the glory of Entgora. And we shall never forget those captured and carried off into slavery. Indeed, on this day, all Entgorans have earned their proper place in the Chronicles of Entgora. From this day forward, today will be remembered as the Second War of the West. And because of this valiant sacrifice, Entgora lives!" The multitude erupted into loud chirps and cheeps and clickity-clacks of approval.

The Queen motioned to quiet the crowds. She continued. "My dear children! Indeed, Entgora not only survives, but thrives! We are not ants who are stuck in past glories or setbacks, but we will rebuild an even stronger Entgora! We will build a new society of black ants, a new black super ant, that is stronger and smarter and that serves Entgora and its righteous Mother even more dutifully!"

More whistles and clickity-clacks of agreement exploded. Some ants jumped up and down in excitement. But Gazer stood in silence.

"My children! Pray silence! To conclude matters, let us now call upon the Great Ant," the white-faced Queen called out as she raised her antennae and forelegs to the sky.

The throng mimicked her movements and listened silently as the Queen intoned, "O Great Ant! Once again we thank thee for thy faithfulness in vanquishing evil from the slopes of Entgora and rewarding the righteous with victory. Let every ant remember how thou bestowed thine wisdom unto the Queen, thine chosen vessel, to give her victory over the evildoers. Now, give her thy blessing to carry forward the glory of Entgora and to make it shine brighter yet. May it be so!"

The Entgorans streamed back into their anthill, confident in the kindly and glorious future of their colony.

But with each step, Gazer's heart sank until she felt it was being trod under her own footsteps.

9

the council of keepers

Gazer staggered back to her group cell, along with several hundred other ants that shared it, to find rest after the harrowing day. It was only mid afternoon, but the frenzied activity of battle made it seem like seasons had passed. Some ants went to sleep straightaway while others nursed their own minor wounds and helped others do the same.

Slowly, she walked through the crowd of ants, meeting eyes with many, greeting each with kindnesses, and stopping here and there to apply saliva to wounds and help some settle into their slumber.

For some reason, other than the clear horrors of war, Gazer felt unsettled deeply. There was something in the way the entire ordeal unfolded. Even the words that Mother spoke did not bring her the kind of joy and confidence that it did to others.

And things troubled her about the trial and about Entgoran colony life. As she surveyed the scene of her tired and injured comrades, questions sprouted in her mind like the Hill of Fatgrass.

Why were the workers placed at the frontline during battle? They surely were not better scrappers than Pokers and Shouters.

And the accused are not provided with a Royal Counsel during trial. Has this always been so?

Why did Mother claim victory, when it was as clear as the Waters of Darktree that the Entmerikans retreated of their own accord, with a large number of Entgoran prisoners at that?

And why does ant kill ant, whether they be Entgoran or Entmerikan...or from another far-off tribe for that matter? Yes, it was true, many Entgorans were taken into captivity and slavery by the Entmerikans—who did seem to her to be quite an evilish lot and perhaps deserving of death—but were the ants that remained in Entgora any less enslaved? Perhaps others were feeling the same things. Nonetheless, she knew these were perilous questions, but she had already asked too many of herself to stop now, whether answers were within antenna reach or not.

Gazer spotted Tenspeed and was thrilled she was spared death. Her friend was injured, and she hurried over to offer aid.

"Tenspeed, my dearest! You're alive! Thank the Great Ant! How are you? What's happened?"

"Ah, Miss Gazer! Thank the Great One indeed. To be sure, these antennae and legs are still twitching. I'm glad you're twitching too, indeed I am."

"Are you hurt badly?" Gazer asked.

"No, no. Don't you be frettin' yourself about me now, Miss Gazer," chirped Tenspeed, "I'll be right as rain soon enough, to be sure."

"At least let me bring you some water so you can wet your jaws a little," Gazer offered.

She scurried over to the chamber's pool of water and sucked up a few drops, carried them back to her friend, and sprayed them into Tenspeed's receiving jaws. Gazer scrutinized her friend's face as she gulped the water greedily. And she knew she could be trusted.

"Tenspeed," Gazer began to whisper cautiously, as she looked around to make sure no ant was spying on their conversation, "can you carry my stone for me to a safe place?"

"Gazer, indeed. You know full well I can keep a secret, especially yours. What is it, pray tell?"

"Do you remember, before the battle, I said something to you?"

"My mind isn't what it used to be, to be sure. I reckon I don't recall. What's troubling you, Gazer?"

"The dream."

"The dream?"

"Yes. The dream I had a few nights ago. I mentioned it to you just before the battle began. Hordes, flowers, and corpses?"

"Ah, yes indeed. Now my mind's clear on it. Well, Miss Gazer, we all have dreams, dare I say frightful ones sometimes, with all manner of the day's doings swirlin' round like—"

"Tenspeed," Gazer interrupted, "this was different and strange."

"Strange? Indeed."

"Yes. It was no common ant dream. It wasn't about the events of the day's duties, like finding food or patching up the hill or being interrogated by Pokers. It wasn't a dream that my own wits contrived. It was about things past, things present, and things that have yet to come to pass."

Gazer searched the chamber once again, her antenna twitching suspiciously, and carried on. "Tenspeed, we will have to speak more of these matters in private. It's not safe here. At least I don't think it is. Not yet, anyway. Let us leave this place. Let us go outside, to the east side of the hill, far from the refuse heap and far from the field of battle. Let's speak no more of this until we're alone."

Tenspeed had never seen her dear friend so troubled and knew she had to go along, if only to comfort her friend's harried mind. They made their way to an exit hole slowly, Tenspeed bracing herself against Gazer the entire way. The duo stopped from time to time to rest one of her sore legs, but they carried on. Gazer felt a measure of guilt at having dragged her

tired friend away from a much-needed rest and, on a few occasions, offered to turn back, but Tenspeed would have none of it. She was determined to learn of her friend's dream. They finally emerged into the cool air, walked to the Field of Yellowgrass, and settled under the shade of the Bloodflower, to the east of Entgora.

"Speak now, Miss Gazer. We are surely alone, no doubt, no doubt, with not an unwelcome twitching antenna in sight. Tell me now of your dream."

"Tenspeed, I had the dream the night before my trial. I found myself in a desert with neither a single creature stirring nor a single plant in sight. And from the distance, an ant walked toward me. When it faced me, I saw it was a female worker ant and wingless. And she wasn't black."

"Well, she's then from another tribe, to be sure. What colour was she then?"

"She was the same as the face pigment the Shouters and

Mother smear on themselves. And the same as that of the ants on the walls in the Hall of Reckoning. Pale white."

"Indeed! This is troublesome news, Miss Gazer, troublesome news, undeniably. More, tell me more of this dream," Tenspeed said impatiently.

"The pale ant sang a song to me," Gazer explained, "but did not uncover its meaning. She said that I must find my own place in the song and help others do the same, but that many would not follow, though they had been called."

"A song? Tell me, tell me the words, the very words, to this song," demanded Tenspeed.

Gazer then recalled the words of the song faithfully and quite readily to her quizzical companion, at times even recreating the complex melody. At other times, the melody escaped her. Tenspeed listened closely, mumbled to herself on occasion, and swirled her antennae in great excitement at the mention of some words. Gazer stopped and then watched her friend survey the dusty ground, whispering to herself.

Gazer broke the silence. "Does it not bode well to dream of such things?"

"I cannot be sure," Tenspeed interjected. "Perhaps good fortune. Perhaps contrariwise. Yes, the reverse, perhaps the reverse, in fact!" Tenspeed shouted and then became quickly sullen. She looked up at the Bloodflower and studied it for a long while, battling within herself between the security of silence and the sting of speech. She finally spoke again.

"Only the Queen and the Shouters, along with a very few, a hidden few, know that the one whom every Entgoran ant calls the Great Ant is also known by another name, a veiled name." Tenspeed paused again and looked at the ground, fearful at the sound of her own words.

Gazer waited patiently for her friend to continue.

"In truth, in truest truth, I shudder at what I reveal to you now," Tenspeed said tersely, "but it seems it is thrust upon me by circumstance. Gazer, the Great Ant in ancient High Entgoran antspeak is known as Byelichkaya, which means Pale White One." Tenspeed was visibly shaken at having shared the hidden name even with this closest of friends.

"Are you sure, Tenspeed?" Gazer asked in a comforting way.

"Yes, oh dear friend Gazer, oh yes, I am surely sure. Indeed, it seems a sure thing that you had a dream of that ancient one, the Great Ant herself! And Miss Gazer, your dream troubles me as much as the curses in the Chronicles of Entgora trouble me. The Curse of Queen Entyaga troubles me, greatly, indeed."

"Curses? Chronicles? But how could you know of such matters, Tenspeed? The sacred words of the Chronicles are forbidden from being taught to workers and males and even Pokers. Only Mother and the Shouters know the words."

"No, no. Not just Mother and the Shouters, to be sure," Tenspeed said gravely. "There are others. There is a group of others, yes, a small band. The Chronicles say that long before you or I were hatched, indeed, and many seasons before even Queen Entvladarka was hatched, some Shouters stirred up strife against their Mother, Queen Entyaga. It is said that these Shouters began to have dreams of a pale white ant. Some thought her to be the Great Ant. No one can say for a certainty. And that pale ant told the Shouters, truly so they claimed, but falsely their Mother claimed, to stir up this strife because their Mother did evil in the sight of the pale ant, evil indeed, great evil, but she could not see her own deeds because her mind was shrouded in shadow. Their Mother banished some from Entgora and executed others, accusing them of being evildoers and dissenters and rebels, preserving the tale as a reminder to all future Queens. Such were the orders of Queen Entyaga. Her final act against them was to decree a curse, a cursed curse to be sure, upon every last one of them.

"And it was these very same Shouters I tell you of now, indeed, who before they were cast out, began to pass on the sacred words of the Chronicles of Entgora to a tiny group of trusted workers and soldiers, a tiny band indeed, who then continued to pass it on to this very day, this very day, today in fact. And I am among this band of Keepers in this ant generation to whom this has been entrusted, although I dared not ever tell you this before for we have taken sacred oaths to secrecy. And the words have been passed on because of the prophecies of the Day of Reckoning, sometimes, yes sometimes, even known as the Day of the Pale White Ant. And the Queens all along the line have known about this day, but have forbidden workers and males and Pokers from knowing of it because, yes, surely yes, because these very same prophecies grasp after the very power of Queens to snatch it away. But I say it all plainly to you now because of what you have told me about your dream. I tell you the solemn truth, the truthful truth, the truest truth, Miss Gazer."

Gazer pulled her one antenna back and dropped her head, unsure of what to make of this tale. Although grieved at the secret that Tenspeed had kept from her for so long, she had known her friend since they were but hatchlings and never had a cause for distrust. Gazer resolved in her mind to believe her words and trust her motives. Gazer straightened herself and then braced her body as if expecting an attack.

"I believe the truth of what you speak. Tell me the words of the curse and the prophecies, Tenspeed. Tell them to me plainly as you have told me everything else plainly this day."

"I will tell you of the cursed curse, indeed, indeed, but the prophecy I will not speak, at least not yet, at least not until things are more clear. Later, perhaps later. Let me speak the whole cursed tale of the cursed curse to you from the Chronicles, so that you grip it with your mind fully. They are ugly words for the most part, to be sure, and I think them an unhappy thing to utter out loud. Yet, I will tell them to you."

Tenspeed shifted uncomfortably, while Gazer waited for her friend to find the right place to start pulling the words from her memory. Finally, Tenspeed's recitation began:

And Queen Entkasha, kindly one
Begat her daughters fair
Three in number, three in favour
Deep in Entgora's lair

Princess Entleo, bravely one
Didst fly to seek fresh fields
In which to birth her colony
And guard it as a shield

Princess Entsofya, wisely one
To knowledge she did kneel
To ev'ry ant of her own tribe
Her light she would reveal

Princess Entyaga, fervent one
Entgora's newest Queen
Didst purify her colony
Of all that was unclean

Great was her zeal for holiness
Great was her hate of sloth
With all her might and majesty
She meted out her wroth

But Shouters they didst stir up strife
Against this noble Queen
And dared to claim the Pale White Ant
Did spake to them in dreams

These wretched fools didst falsely say
The Pale One said by night
That Queen Entyaga's noble reign
Was evil in her sight

Deceitful rebels conjured lies
And made the anthill drink
From all their pools of treachery
And blasphemy and stink

Thus Queen Entyaga banished them
For all that they had durst
Then on these Shouters she decreed
This solemn royal curse

Cursed be the Shouter's dream
Cursed be their cause
Cursed be their fellowship
Cursed be their laws

Cursed be the hour they rise
Cursed be their rest
Cursed be the roads they walk
Cursed be their jest

Cursed be their new hatchlings
Cursed be their eggs
Cursed be their antennae
Cursed be their legs

Cursed be from this day forth
All ants who heed their shams
And claim to dream their darkish dreams
May they be henceforth damned

Give heed to me, all unborn Queens
Give heed if thou wilt rise
For you to reign in victory
All rebel ants must die

Tenspeed sighed as the last few words departed her jaws. Gazer had never heard these ancient words before, so fiercely darkish were they. The message was clear. And she was afraid. And her body began to shiver. Tenspeed was weary. The pair was pondering the same question, but in the solitude of their own thoughts: What was to be done now?

"Miss Gazer," began Tenspeed cautiously, "we must take the message of your dream to the council of the Keepers, indeed, with no sideways thinkings or doings. We can discuss its meaning then, to be sure, and decide on what should be done. We cannot, no, could not, should not, will not, decide anything now. Keep the words spoken here hidden until I come for you. In the meanwhile, we keep to our antish business. Indeed, swear it! Indeed, vow to it!"

Gazer nodded in agreement. The pair returned to the anthill, not speaking a word to each other along the way, trading glances only a few times.

The days that followed were filled with the routine duties of an ant. Taking refuse to the rubbish pile. Collecting food bits from the outside. Repairing damaged walls. A large priority was placed on nursing ants that had been wounded in the Second War of the West. Both Tenspeed and Gazer launched themselves into their duties with special vigour, hoping perhaps to soothe the inner conflict and worry that were aroused because of their conversation. And they made sure they spent no time in each other's company to avert any suspicion. Gazer was secretly hoping that somehow she might not need to meet with the Keepers and that Tenspeed would deal with these matters on her own. After all, Gazer asked not to become a dreamer, and she knew nothing of the Chronicles of Entgora, except for what she had only just learned. But the day of meeting was sure to come, sooner or later. And, when Tenspeed was given the call herself from another Keeper, she went straightaway to Gazer.

"Miss Gazer," Tenspeed said as she tapped the top of Gazer's head with an antenna to get her friend's attention, "the time has come. It's upon us. Indeed, the time is right now, in fact."

"Ah, I was daring to hope that you would forget me on account of your busyness. It's now, is it? Right now?" Gazer asked as Tenspeed nodded. "Well then, dear friend, let us go to meet your friends—and I hope mine—to see what wisdom they might impart."

"No more words," Tenspeed said gravely.

Tenspeed motioned for Gazer to follow her down a corridor. They moved swiftly into an unfinished section of the colony that, apart from a few work crews here and there going about their business, was completely empty. The duo finally arrived at their destination and entered a chamber. Gazer guessed that there were maybe thirty ants gathered there, mostly workers but also a few soldiers, both Pokers and Shouters, and some males. There were no familiar faces to Gazer, except Digdirt who, along with Tenspeed, rescued her from ruin in the last war. Every ant stood quietly, as if in deep thought or meditation, although a few whispers and cheerful greetings were exchanged. It was a solemn but joyful group. They remained still until all the expected attendees had arrived. Then, to Gazer's surprise, one of the workers—rather than one of the Shouters—opened the meeting.

"Friends," began the worker ant grandly, "thank you for coming again to this meeting of the Keepers. Let us begin by seeking wisdom."

At this, some ants raised their antennae to the sky, while others bowed their heads.

"O Great Ant, great is thy name. Caress our minds with thine antennae of wisdom and strength. Protect us from the usual distractions of antish life so we can hear clearly the words to be spoken. Protect us from being discovered by the long antennae of the enemy. Help us discover thy will for us. And give us fortitude to act upon it. May it be so."

The other ants echoed "May it be so."

The worker continued. "I see we have one new ant joining us today. Warmth to you," the worker said as she motioned with her antennae to Gazer, who shrank back a little but acknowledged the others with a nod.

"Who vouches for our guest?" asked another worker suspiciously.

"I vouch for this ant," Tenspeed answered. "This ant is trustworthy, indeed, indeed. I vow to it."

"Well, then, you are surely welcome," added one of the Shouters.

"Sisters," injected one of the Pokers, "for the sake of our new friend, let us give our names." All agreed this was a goodly act of courtesy. Then round the circle the gathered made their names known to Gazer.

"Tenspeed," began Flick, a worker known for tapping her antennae together nervously at even the smallest sign of trouble, "as the vouching ant, tell us why you invited your friend, Gazer, to the meeting of the Keepers."

"Sisters! Gazer has been my friend since we were young, indeed, since we were hatchlings. And I have been faithful, faithful in fact, to my vow as a Keeper to speak to no unworthy ant, not even one odd seeming ant, about our sisterhood. But, but, but," began Tenspeed excitedly, suddenly curbing her verve with caution, "then Gazer, truly, had a dream. A dream about a pale white ant."

Some of the ants were visibly intrigued, taking a step forward, while others swayed their heads askance.

"Yes, in fact, sisters, this is true I say," Tenspeed added. "And words were spoken by a pale ant to my dear friend Gazer, standing here before you. Words I want you to hear and judge for yourselves."

"Gazer, can you tell us of this dream and the words you heard? In some detail, if you please," a Poker named Whistler inquired. Whistler was esteemed by the council for her charisma and skill in speech.

"Yes, yes, I can," Gazer began nervously. "It was an odd dream. I understand it not. So I can only describe it for you. In my dream, there was a desert. Empty. Nothing in sight. No smells that my antennae could sense. And I was standing in the middle of it. Then from a long way off, an ant walked towards me. And when it came up to me, to my very face, I saw that it was a worker ant. A pale white worker ant."

More interest grew noticeably among Gazer's hearers. Some muttering sounds were made, whether of approval or dismay no one could tell. Gazer paused.

"Please sister, continue with your tale," encouraged Flick.

Tenspeed tapped her friend's back encouragingly.

Gazer breathed deeply and then carried on. "Then, sisters, the ant sang me a song. Whether a dreadful or blissful song I cannot tell, though I sing it for you now."

Gazer then sang the dream song to the Keepers. With each turn of phrase, she could see the growing agitation of some. A few scratched their heads softly with their antennae, while others swayed slowly to the melody. What most were thinking, though, she could not surmise from their stunned countenance. As she finally came to the end of it, she felt this was just the beginning of something else, as yet unknown. The eyes of all were on Gazer. And a silence fell upon the chamber.

Tenspeed stirred the stillness. "Truly, verily, sisters, this is one and the same song that Gazer recounted to me only a few days before today. And now you hear it for yourselves, in fact, in your own hearing. And you are witnesses yourselves that this ant, who is no Keeper to be sure, I vouch it, was given the very words of the Chronicle prophecy in her dream. And I can see that many of you are moved, but to what end I dare not guess, indeed."

"Yes, yes, sister Tenspeed," interjected Whistler, "we are moved, greatly moved, as you say. But we are concerned, too, that the words of the Chronicles have found their way into uninitiated jaws. Did you not learn these words of foretelling, Gazer, not from a dream, but rather from your friend Tenspeed?"

"And why would the Great Ant come in a dream to an ant who is no Keeper?" blurted one of the ants. "Are we not worthy ourselves to receive such dreams?"

"No, no," Tenspeed protested, "I surely never betrayed my oath as a Keeper. Verily, I never told the words of any prophecy in the Chronicles nor did I let one word escape my jaws about being a Keeper except, that is, just a few days ago. These words came to Gazer in a dream, just as she told you. I swear it."

"So she says! But how do we know that she is no spy sent by the enemy to scurry in amongst us?" proposed Whistler. "Perhaps this Gazer sheared off her own antenna to fit the prophecy and was taught its words by the Shouters. The enemy's antenna is long, and we may all be in grave danger!"

Others voiced their agreement with cries of "Here, here!" and "Surely!"

"My missing antenna?" Gazer whispered to Tenspeed amidst the growing noise. "What has that to do with anything?"

"Please, sisters, wait!" interrupted Flick. "Let's not be rash. Let's not be hasty. We have heard our sister ant speak. Think on it well. How could the enemy fix in our midst a spy if we have kept true to our oath as Keepers? And even if the enemy has discovered that we exist, by some trickery, why have we survived for so long without banishment or execution?"

"Ah," countered Whistler, "but do the Eight Leggys not patiently wait and wait and wait for their prey to come to their webby lair until *zomp!* it suddenly gets trapped in the web's stickiness, only to await its doom? Let's not forget the enemy's craftiness!"

"Sister," challenged Digdirt, known for habitually

scratching the ground with her forelegs when engaged in a battle of the wills, "all things are possible, as you say. But what is the true likelihood that such a scheme has been hatched by the enemy? What's more, you know the other prophecy as well as any ant here, Whistler. Has it escaped your memory? Let me lay it back into your mind again." So Digdirt intoned,

> *Count the hours till freedom reigns*
> *Count the days till evil wanes*
> *Count the nights till justice wins*
> *Count the seasons and the winds*
> *Count the elders and the young*
> *Count the ant with all but one*

"'Tis true enough, Digdirt, indeed," Tenspeed said, with a seriousness unusual to her. "The prophecy bids us take heed of a seven-limbed ant, to be sure. What ant, even in some crazed antish moment, would sever her own limb on purpose especially, says I, to try by some trick to fulfill a prophecy she was not even privy to? To me, even me myself, the matter is as clear as the Waters of Darktree. I invoke my right as a Keeper to put the council to the open vote. Where does the matter stand with you, sisters?"

Flick, Digdirt, and most of the other Keepers agreed openly with Tenspeed that the dream was genuine and now looked on Gazer with great affection. They had settled in their minds that the prophecies were indeed coming to pass. A few others, like Whistler, were still unsure and voted against Gazer and did not even trust her with a half measure, still musing that she might be a spy or had gone mad.

"Then the matter is settled and closed!" began Ramhead, the worker who opened the meeting at the start. "The great majority of the council has openly declared that Gazer's dream is genuine and that you, Gazer, are no spy. You are now to be known as official 'Friend' to the Keepers. And as a friend you may, if you so wish, enter into a period of learning in the words of the Chronicles and the ways of the Keepers, to become a Keeper yourself after the completion of your novitiate."

Gazer thought for some moments before she spoke. "I hope I can be a good friend to the council. Thank you for bestowing such an honour on me. And, yes, I am keen to become a Keeper."

"If the sisterhood permits," Tenspeed interjected, "I myself, truly, would like to apprentice our new friend in the ways of the Keepers and in the deep knowledge of the Pale One."

"It is your right, sister," added Digdirt firmly, looking about the room to stave off any possible objections that might be advanced.

"Now then," Ramhead suggested, "let us embrace our new friend." The council crowded around Gazer and tapped her one antenna affectionately, as well as drumming her lightly on the head and torso. Whistler and the few that were still leery did so as well, for the decision was now official. They would keep their reservations to themselves until an opportune time.

"Sisters, now that we know the prophecy is unfolding in our generation, what is to be done?" asked Ramhead.

"As you all know," said Stony, "the words of the Chronicles do not tell us what is to be done, not exactly in any case. This has always been a matter of controversy throughout the Keeper generations among some. But I think I have the mind of the Great One, when I say that every Entgoran ant, whether worker or Poker or male or Shouter, needs to know that she is coming! Does not another prophecy say as much?"

Stony then recited a brief passage from the Chronicles to make her point.

Blessed be the valleys
And happy be the hills
Goodly be the daughters
Not found standing still

For justice roars like waters
Rushing from on high
And wisdom falls like raindrops
Ploughing through the sky

Keep awake, O daughters
Do not confer with fear
For she whose limbs are restless
Is coming and is near

"Sisters," added Flick, "I, too, like most of you, have always understood this passage as a prophecy of her return. And as her daughters, I believe the hour has come for the others to know she is coming!" Almost all the others voiced their agreement heartily and began to chirp and whistle loudly.

"Please, please, sisters," said Ramhead, interrupting the din, "we must exercise great caution. The enemy is strong and would snatch away our very lives. Then we are agreed on what should be done. Indeed, let every ant know she is coming. But do it secretly. Do it safely. Do not throw your shiny stones before beasts, lest you yourselves be trampled underfoot. Greet every ant with the words 'She is coming.' No more. No less. You are sent out as ants among the beasts. Carry these tidings to all Entgorans everywhere. Complete your task. In the powerful name of *Byelichkaya,* our blessed Pale White Ant, go in peace."

The chamber fell eerily silent, and the ants departed slowly in ones and pairs along diverse paths into the darkness of the corridors, not knowing what lay ahead.

And from that day forward, Gazer grew in wisdom and in wordcraft and in the ways of the Keepers.

10

the revolt

The Keepers were now charged with a new mission given them by providence, that of taking the message "She is coming!" to Entgora. It was not an easy task to embrace, for they had been an unknown society for many generations and knew not any other way of life. But now their mandate required them to step out of their solitude and break their silence. How could they achieve their task without being discovered by the enemy, who knew more than many suspected and would surely banish or execute them? Moreover, was it not, in fact, presumption on their part to even begin to spread their message to the entire mass of Entgoran ants, almost one hundred and twenty thousand strong in all?

But, begin they did.

During the next season, Entgorans went about their usual business. Collecting food. Repairing leaks. Finishing construction projects. Raising young hatchlings in antish ways and teaching them antspeak. And heaping their aged dead onto the refuse pile outside.

All the while, the society of Keepers was spreading their message from antenna-to-antenna and ant-to-ant, quietly, slowly, and carefully. They took their news to males and females, workers and soldiers, Pokers and Shouters all. Their only words were "She is coming!" They dared not explain more for fear of the enemy. Most ants did not understand—nor did they care to—for being ants they had more important things to do, like go about their antish tasks. Some mocked and sneered and derided the messengers as mutterers and mumblers and thought it a peculiar thing that a fellow ant would speak words to them that made no apparent sense and had no practical meaning. Others were excited and curious enough to inquire after the meaning of these strange words, but their enthusiasm waned when no satisfactory explanation was readily forthcoming.

Yet a few, a happy few, were captivated by the unusual tidings, inquiring of the bearers of the words tirelessly until the Keepers relented and explained the message more fully though only, as it were, in stealth. It started small, but as the number of devoted inquirers grew into the thousands and their hunger for knowledge increased, some of the Keepers taught the very words of the Chronicles to these new followers, calling them "Friends" and sending them in ones and pairs also to spread the words of her coming.

Thus did the veiled name of *Byelichkaya,* the Pale White One, become known among new believers. Many Entgorans—both mockers and inquirers—were even beginning to have dreams of the Pale White Ant, who spoke no words, disturbing the unconvinced and comforting the converted. In this manner did the tidings reach much of Entgora.

But the antennae of the enemy were long, and few things escaped her notice. The words "She is coming!" reached the Queen herself and her inner circle of Shouters. And the words greatly distressed her, for she also knew the words of the prophecies. The time had come for a masterstroke. And in her wrath she moved swiftly.

"Royal Soldiers," began Queen Entvladarka, "loyal ones, beloved children, disturbing words have reached me of a group of troublemakers who stir up my daughters throughout this holy realm. These deceitful workers spread rumours and fables and twist the words of the Chronicles for their own ends. In doing so, they prove themselves blasphemers and rebels. Cherished Royal Soldiers, you yourselves have been taught the words of the Chronicles and are guardians of it. These dreamers—so let them be called—profess to have seen the Pale White One, our beloved Great Ant, in night visions. In the futility of their minds, they further warp the sacred words by claiming that the prophecies speak of the downfall of Queens. These upstarts would seek to rob me of my motherhood and destroy a civilization that was established many generations ago in another age. False teachers easily convince unlearned minds of their sacrilege and are now the scourge of Entgora, with thousands of followers. And you all know the curses pronounced by my royal ancestor, Queen Entyaga, on those ants in her generation who indulged in such scheming and trickery and would not be swayed from their path. Let her counsel be our guide in this hour of trial. Entgora must be purged of this evil at all costs. I now solemnly invoke the Edict of Entyaga. Royal Soldiers, I grant you emergency powers to act without official royal consent. Do what seems most needful to you. Do all at will. From ant to ant and chamber to chamber, use whatever means necessary. Arrest. Imprison. Interrogate. Torment. Only hearken to this rule of thirds. Let one third recant. Let one third be banished. Let one third be executed. Since these rebels sow seeds of false hope, let them also reap their just destiny! Let the great cleansing commence. And may the Great Ant be with you in this holy cause!"

And so it began, to the ruin of many.

The Shouters, numbering a thousand strong, left their Hollow and flowed like a mighty river through the passageways of the colony, rushing from cell to cell and level to level in search of the Keepers and their Friends, all now mockingly called Dreamers. They used the same scheme over and over. Entering each chamber, they placed a goodly number of guards at each entrance to prevent escape and tortured some of the youngish and oldish ants in the sight of all, demanding confessions from the group upon pain of death.

"In the name of the Queen!" the Shouters would declare. "Which of you are blasphemous Dreamers, claiming to have seen the Pale Ant in night visions? Which of you have poisoned the colony with the words 'She is coming'? Come now, confess or your sisters shall meet their end! Those who give us the names of these evildoers will be rewarded with the choicest of foods and better working conditions. And you will be spared the righteous wrath of the Queen. In the name of the Great Ant, save yourselves from this perversion and prove yourselves loyal to your kind!"

In this manner was great dissension stirred up in the colony. Some ants betrayed their fellow ants as Dreamers for the sake of personal gain and salvation and joined with the Shouters in searching out the so-named traitors. Many under torture or to stop the anguish of others confessed they had seen the Pale One in the night or had believed the words, "She is coming." These were either executed on the spot or tormented further until they recanted, being conscripted by force into the Shouter army.

The bolder of the Keepers and Friends, though, continued spreading their message of the Pale One's return in the face of great danger, drawing over to their following a growing number of ants. But many, Dreamer and non-believer alike, seeing the cruelty of their Mother, waged battle against the Shouters, overtaking them and fleeing for their lives, vowing to overthrow the tyrant and establish a new order in Entgora. A warning was sounded throughout the anthill that a great cleansing was at hand. All was chaos. Much blood was spilt. Many fled the colony. Most plotted revenge.

Yet the Dreamer following grew.

As for those who remained to fight against the Queen,

they organized an army after the fashion of the Queen's army. They appointed for themselves a Poker ant named Cruncher, known for crunch-a-munching her food and words vigorously, as their Queen. She chose for herself a fiercely loyal inner circle of twelve captains, mostly soldiers along with a few workers like Buzzjaw and Shooter, each of whom had a legion of ants under their command. They called themselves The Entgoran Ants Liberation Army, whose motto was "Death to the villain! A free Entgora for all!" Their sole purpose was the overthrow of Queen Entvladarka and her minions and the installment of Cruncher as the new Queen. From cell to cell and level to level, they gave fight and laid victorious siege to the lowest underground levels, amounting to a goodly one third of the entire anthill. Such was the militant discipline and unquestioning allegiance to Cruncher that underlings who lost heart in the fight or disobeyed direct orders were executed. The fate of deserters was worse. They were captured, humiliated publicly, tortured, and ultimately slain. Theirs was a holy revolution, and no anti-revolt would be tolerated.

As for those who survived the exterminations and fled Entgora, they did so in the thousands, streaming from their home in a long caravan to the south. Some ran. Some walked. Some limped. And many wept as they entered the wild under the open sky...among them Gazer, Tenspeed, Digdirt, Flick, and Whistler from the band of Keepers. Ramhead was among the faithful that were massacred.

The pilgrims travelled some distance to seek shelter in the hollow of a felled tree trunk, within eye range of Entgora. They called their home the Exodus Tree. They sojourned there for some days, nursing the wounded and weary and comforting the distraught. They foraged for food, finding an abundance of small berries and water nearby. Sentinels were posted all round the tree, the better part of them on the side facing Entgora. Scouts were sent to spy on their old home and its goings on, ensuring that no raiding bands of Queen Entvladarka's troops were sent to attack them.

Amidst all this, every ant knew that their lives had changed eternally—whether for the better or contrariwise, none were sure.

11

the new society

Some weeks after the great cleansing, peace descended on the Exodus Tree. Now free of the tyrant Queen and her cronies, the refugee ants were breathing the free air, working together side by side without fear of domination and control. Each ant knew what needed to be done and went about her or his antish business with zest and joy. Minor disputes occasionally arose between some ants over food and work distribution, but were dealt with quickly and to the satisfaction of all by a group of twelve wise Reckoners—among them Whistler and Flick—appointed by the ants themselves.

After a season, many began to ask when their new colony would build their own anthill, not only for protection from the elements and beasts, but also for the unity and stability it would offer. And of greater importance, the question circulated among many as to when they would appoint their own Queen. Some, though, were unconvinced that such things from the old order should be resurrected among them. Quarrels arose about these matters, so much so that it reached the antennae of the Reckoners, who discussed these things amongst themselves for some time before calling a public assembly of all ants to settle these affairs officially. As the masses rallied together, the Reckoners perched themselves in the sight of all on a tree branch lying on the ground.

"Fellow ants! Sisters! Comrades!" began Strongleg, a Poker

ant who was one of the Reckoners. "We are gathered here today as one body of ants. We have survived the purges of the evil Queen Entvladarka. We have fled together, bled together, and wept together. Just as we have a common heritage, so too do we have a common future. We have been living, working, sharing, and playing together now for a season with equality, freedom, and unity. We are all being schooled in the sacred words of the Chronicles, which brings us closer to each other and the Great Ant. In this spirit, let us resolve the disputations that have arisen among us."

The mass of ants chirped and whistled and clickity-clacked their jaws in approval at the words spoken. Gazer and her friends joined in heartily, glad that their friend Flick was in such a place of influence.

"It has reached our attention," interjected another Reckoner, who was a worker ant named Twitch. As the clamour died down, she continued. "It has reached our attention that the cross words spoken among you have to do with the erection of an anthill, a permanent new home for our new colony. My sisters and I have considered this matter at length," she said as she motioned to the other Reckoners. "We all agree that we cannot stay in Exodus Tree forever. We are in danger from weather and beasts, and we must have a safe place to raise new hatchlings. The young are the future. And we must declare to all the glorious new society that we build. What better way to do this than by the witness of a new anthill in the sight of all, including Queen Entvladarka and Old Entgora. Perhaps our example will sway them from their evil path. Therefore, we declare to you with the authority you have bestowed on us, that such an anthill will indeed be constructed! Long live New Entgora!"

At the sound of the words "New Entgora," the mass of ants leapt and danced with joy. Flick motioned for the crowds to quiet down. Gazer, Tenspeed, and Digdirt watched their friend gladly, straining to hear her words.

"Sisters! Sisters!" shouted Flick over the still noisy rally. "Indeed, long live New Entgora! Along with my fellow Reckoners and yourselves, I too am pleased at this decision and look forward to the day when we can all sleep soundly in our chambers. But, let us not forget that it was not many days before that we did not sleep soundly at all. Some of our sisters who believed the words of the Pale One's coming were murdered in their sleep or driven out in the still of the night. The words of our sister Strongleg are true. We must always keep before our eyes equality, freedom, and unity; otherwise we have nothing. Therefore, it is our judgment that each chamber of one hundred ants in the New Entgora will elect from among themselves two Proxy ants that will meet with the ruling council of the Reckoners to voice the concerns of the common ant. Moreover, when a Reckoner dies or is too oldish or becomes corrupt, they will be replaced by another with a reputation for wisdom and character and skill. And you yourselves will have the power to submit the names of such ants to us in the ruling council. And in our wisdom and by the authority you have given to us, we will make the final selection. Our colony will be a new society of the ant, for the ant, and by the ant. Your voice will be heard in the New Entgora!"

Much loud rejoicing followed. Never had such a thing been heard among antkind. None assembled could have imagined in their wildest ant dreams that they would live to see such days of freedom. Gazer and her friends were glad at much of what their comrade Flick had said. But though they pondered her words carefully, they could not reconcile themselves whole-heartedly to them. Their unnamed uneasiness was soon to plainly manifest itself.

Whistler then stood tall and raised her antennae and forelegs until the crowds settled themselves. Whistler was older than many of the other Reckoners and was possessed of a regal look. Her words carried great weight among the council, for she was very wise indeed and gave great heed to the whims and opinions of the masses. And, as Gazer learned during the council of the Keepers, Whistler was also skilled in wordcraft.

"New Entgorans," began Whistler in a low soft tone, "in my days not so long ago as a loyal member of the council of Keepers, I learned and studied and devoted myself to the words of the Chronicles. But I did so with a feeling of great sadness and solemnity. Every day I would turn in the direction of the rising light and meditate on the holy words and ask the Great Ant to lift my sorrowful heart. Why was I in such anguish, you may ask? For your sake, my dear sisters! Yes, for your sake! Every day when I gazed at the words of the Chronicles, I knew that you yourselves, my fellow ants, borne of the same womb as I, were robbed of their beauty. Yes, my dear compatriots, you were ignorant, blind, poor, and starving! Ignorant of the heritage of antkind and of the future that could be yours! Blind to your own darkness and to the shining light that could guide you along the path on your march to freedom! Poor and in need of the riches that could purchase your rightful destiny! Starving for the nourishment that could make you strong and powerful! But that day is over, and the age of the ordinary ant is now upon us!"

The masses roared and cheered and whistled and chirped, moved at the words. Whistler surveyed the crowds and waved to them with both forelegs. She let the rally rejoice until it quieted of its own accord. Whistler then continued, but now with a growing fervency in her voice and ever grander gestures.

"My fellow ants, I ask you now, at whose feet do we lay the blame for such a long age of injustice? Are your six feet to be laden with guilt for not grasping after your rightful place and power? No, indeed not! The enslaved are not responsible for their own slavery! Well then, do we lay blame at the feet of the Keepers for not delivering the holy words of freedom to you earlier? No, indeed not! The sower of seeds cannot hasten the day of harvest! Peradventure, do some of you even harbour doubts about the righteousness of the Great Pale Ant for delaying your emancipation? No, indeed not! The rescuer deserves only high reverence from the rescued! My sisters, the charge of crimes against antkind cannot, should not, and will not be smeared on the faces of ants, the Keepers, or the Pale One! The charge of high treason, rather, must tarnish the face of that despot Queen Entvladarka and her underlings!"

The multitude once again erupted. Violence was in the air, and words of revenge were on many a jaw. Some loudly pronounced curses on their former Mother and Queen. Some called for the death of the fat bully, while others wished to witness the plucking out of her antennae and legs. Many, though, like Gazer and her friends, were not brimming with vengeance, but were rather glad at their good fortune at having lived to see this day of liberty.

"Ants of New Entgora!" Whistler now bellowed, blowing the spark into a flame. "Your freedom is ever in danger as long as Queen Entvladarka breathes and moves. Your liberty is in jeopardy as long as her underlings scurry and scamper about, looking for an ant to devour. Your emancipation dangles over the chasm of slavery as long as you remain divided. What is to be done, my friends? We must hearken to the lessons of the past if we are to live triumphantly in the future. Let me remind you of the common antish proverb that says that, 'The ant who looks behind her to see the face of her pursuer must watch her steps lest she fall into a ditch.' More importantly, let us look to the holy example set before us in the Chronicles. You yourselves know that the holy record recounts the history of past generations of antkind and how every colony that has thrived and survived and stepped confidently into tomorrow has been a united colony. Equality! Freedom! Unity! These remain mere words if our new way of life cannot be guarded from those who would destroy us. And there is only one way to protect our New Entgora and our most cherished values and dreams. My friends, we must appoint for ourselves a new Queen!"

The roar from the thousands gathered now was deafening. Most ants were in a frenzy. Cheers and whistles and chirps and clicks reverberated between heaven and earth. Ants began to chant in unison "We want a Queen!" and "Whistler for Queen!"

But a small number of ants was pierced to the quick. Gazer was compelled by some inner force to speak to the masses, but she was a long way off from the felled tree branch where the Reckoners were perched.

An idea burst within her mind. She needed the aid of her friends. Amidst the festive atmosphere, Digdirt braced her body while Tenspeed climbed onto her. Gazer then made her way up to the very top of the ant wall, steadying herself on Tenspeed. She waved her one antenna and forelegs frantically, chirping and cheeping overtop the throng of ants. This odd sight quickly drew the attention of onlookers. The Reckoners motioned to Gazer, Flick beckoning the crowds to quiet down. Whistler shifted uncomfortably at seeing the ant with one antenna again.

"Sisters! Sisters!" began Gazer. "Please indulge me in speaking with you for a few moments. Friends, I am a simple worker ant like many of you. I am not as brave as many of the former Shouters and Pokers among us, nor am I as learned as those who have been faithful Keepers of the Chronicles for many a season, nor am I as skilled in the craft of words as the council of Reckoners, especially its foremost member, Whistler. Even so, please heed carefully the words I say to you this day."

"I am overjoyed that we stand free of the tyranny of Queen Entvladarka and her rabble of followers and are far removed from the civil war waged in Old Entgora by Cruncher and her band of warriors. We are now living and toiling in peace shoulder to shoulder, helping each other with the skills and talents that we each possess to create a New Entgora worthy of the sacrifices made by so many. We are indeed one body. And for that we have just cause to rejoice. Moreover, I am pleased that the words *equality, freedom,* and *unity* have been spoken several times today and lifted up as the basic building stones for our new society. I, too, believe that these are mere words if they are not cherished and preserved and lived out practically day to day and ant to ant."

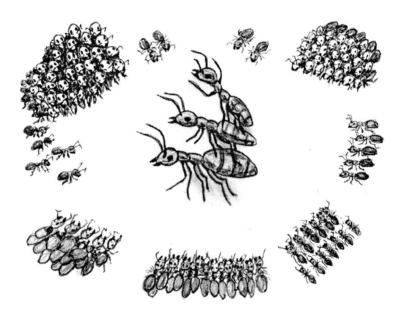

"Sisters, many days ago I had a dream of the Pale White Ant who sang to me a song. Only later while meeting with the council of Keepers, did I learn that these were passages from the holy Chronicles themselves. Yes, as many of you know and can see for yourselves, I am the ant with one antenna who was prophesied long ago to first bring the tidings of the return of the Pale One, to make straight and smooth her holy path. Of these matters the council of Keepers are witnesses, many of whom are still alive and among us, including the esteemed Reckoners Flick and Whistler. And this has been noised abroad and is no secret to you. I say this not to heap on myself any great name, but only that you may hearken to my words more carefully. Indeed, the Pale One must increase. I have already decreased. And we must all decrease and walk in humility. The old order must be washed away. And so it should be. Let me remind you of the sacred words which tell us plainly that, 'The order soon will sleep in death, its corpse shall stink and spoil. The head and tail will change their place, till ev'ry ant be royal.' And the holy words speak even with dire warning that, 'The meek shall then inherit earth and flee the coming fall.'

"Sisters, how then shall we live? True equality, freedom, and unity are always in danger whenever some ants are the head and others the tail. So, I tell you this. Do not call any ant mother, for you are all sisters. And do not call any ant master, for you are to serve one another without preference. And do not call any ant leader, for one is your leader: the Pale White Ant. And are not the titles of Queen, Reckoner, and even Proxy, merely different words for head? And are not the vast majority of you then the tail, being wagged to and fro at another's whim?"

Alas, most ants did not take kindly to these criticisms and made unpleasant hissing sounds. Some even chomped at the ground violently. Gazer and her friends were somewhat afraid but were not surprised at the displeasure shown her. Gazer saw the Reckoners conferring amongst themselves. Flick tapped her antennae together nervously as she and Whistler launched into an especially animated debate with each other. One of the Reckoners unknown to Gazer moved forward a few steps, motioned for the crowd to calm down, and shouted, "Carry on, Gazer! Make your thoughts fully known!"

"Thank you," started Gazer. "Thank you for permitting my

voice to be heard. Sisters, I plead with you that you do not misunderstand my meaning. Know that I say these things because my antenna embraces you all and all that we have built together. But I must speak some more things to you that you may not bear well. Give heed to this warning. You yourselves know the way of a Queen. She will heap on her head great titles like Grand Mother, High Guardian, Mighty Warrior, Just Lawgiver, and True Interpreter of the Chronicles. She will eat the choicest of foods, live in the largest of chambers, and be the only ant in the entire colony whose loins are fertile so as to have offspring. She will take her daughters and do many a thing that will usurp equality, freedom, and unity. She will appoint for herself, or peradventure allow you to appoint, an inner ruling council of masters—whom you now call Reckoners—to consult with her to make her grip on the realm stronger.

"She will assign for herself, or perchance allow you to elect, a group of leaders—whom you now call Proxies—of hundreds and fifties and tens to ensure that all ants do her bidding. She will see to it that her servants collect food, feed her hatchlings, erect an anthill, defend the colony from enemies, and wage war on other ant tribes to gain wealth, land, and glory. But she herself will do none of this work, and her antennae and legs will not be muddy from toil or soiled with blood. And she will punish any who stray from this path and all who are free-thinkers and free-doers. When you choose masters to rule over you, verily, verily, you reject the rightful rule of the Pale One herself. Then you will cry out in that day to the Great Pale Ant because of your Queen whom you have chosen for yourselves and because of the Reckoners and the Proxies, but you will not hear an answer and no rescue will come!"

"This ant would make herself Queen!" came a cry somewhere from the throng of ants. Angry and loud hisses and chirps of disapproval were heard. Great disputations arose between the majority who disagreed with Gazer and the small minority that felt she was in the right. There was some pushing and jostling, antenna against antenna and body against body, but no deadly violence.

Gazer, discouraged and afraid, jumped down from the perch made by Tenspeed and Digdirt, falling to the ground. As she was pulled to her feet by Digdirt, some formed a wall around her to defend against possible attempts on her life.

Soon the throng was chanting over and over again, "Give us a Queen! Give us Whistler! Down with the radicals!"

The Reckoners were visibly unnerved at the unrest. They circled together and argued busily amongst themselves for some time. Then their circle broke. Whistler stepped forward on the tree branch, stood tall, surveyed the masses, and basked for a few moments in the words of the mantra before speaking. She motioned to the masses for attention until there was almost absolute silence.

"Friends," Whistler said commandingly, "you will have your Queen!"

The crowds let out a loud united cheer. "Hurrah, hurrah, hurrah!"

"Sisters," Whistler began again, "you will have your Queen and your Reckoners and your Proxies to ensure your equality, freedom, and unity. The Reckoners and I agree with our sister Gazer's words that the corruption of leaders has been the downfall of many an ant and many an anthill. We make the solemn promise to you that we will do all in our power to guarantee that such a beastly beast does not show its vile head among us. Corruption will be crushed!

"However, we do not agree that mothers and masters and leaders are evil in themselves. For who will guide and protect New Entgora? Our colony cannot be of two opinions. If we Reckoners are right, then follow us. If sister Gazer is right, then follow her. We, therefore, with all good will and in good faith, invite all who agree with sister Gazer to follow her to begin a new colony of their own. No harm shall come to you if you choose this path. Please, sister Gazer, lead your ants!"

And so was New Entgora divided into two realms. Knowing they had no other recourse, Gazer, Tenspeed, and Digdirt made their way slowly through the masses in a south-easterly direction. But the trio did not do so alone. For out of the multitude of ants emerged ones and twos and threes and fours, here and there, far and wide, who followed in the trio's footsteps, flowing out of the huddled body of ants like blood streaming from a wounded beast. Some heckled them as traitors and rebels, but all in all it was a peaceful departure. And many, in fact, wept. All told, only five hundred of the three thousand ants accompanied Gazer.

As for New Entgora, the next few seasons were ones of great activity. A new anthill near the Exodus Tree was constructed to accommodate ten thousand ants in hopes of future growth, with further expansion plans in view. The usual antish techniques, materials, and layout after the standard fashions were used. Individual chambers were hollowed to house one hundred ants and were named cloisters. Many prison cells too were built to detain and retrain future dissenters, of which there were a goodly number. The earth around the anthill was sloped, and a trench was dug round about to draw any heavy rainfall.

Their new home was impressive indeed, being only a miniature version of the cone-shaped glory of Old Entgora. All took part in the work, even the leaders. The ants swelled with pride at their achievement. And as promised, each cloister could elect two Proxy ants to represent them and their concerns when they met with the ruling council of twelve Reckoners, who held their position for life unless extraordinary circumstances dictated otherwise.

And to everyone's delight, Whistler was indeed appointed the first Queen of New Entgora. Orders were given by Queen Whistler to have the words *Equality, Freedom,* and *Unity* etched in ancient High Entgoran on the walls of each cloister just below her own image. Most ants, though, could not even read the olden script, but its delicate features amused and delighted them. Sentinels were placed on constant lightrise-to-lightdown watch, being especially suspicious of the goings on in Old Entgora. Occasional skirmishes happened between the neighbours when they accidentally ventured too far into the other's territory, but only one costly battle over boundaries was ever fought over the next several seasons.

As for the small company that accompanied Gazer, Tenspeed, and Digdirt, they settled southeast of New Entgora within eye view of it. They too built a new home, but it was not after the usual fashion of the ants of Old or New Entgora with their masters and thralls. All laboured jointly, as far as age, strength, and health permitted. Daily the ants organized themselves into sundry work groups of Twiggers, Diggers, Stonerollers, Lifters,

Carriers, Levellers, Dirtmasters, Scroungers, Dunkers, Leafbearers, Fetchers, Feeders, Foragers, Hatchlingwatchers, and the like.

And thus did they build a vast underground network of chambers that could each house twenty to thirty ants at the most. Each chamber was considered a complete ant colony unto itself and was called so. Each had its own holeway to the ground surface for its members to roam freely in and out. These were not guarded. And the small colonies were not joined to one another directly, but each colony had its own pathway leading to two much larger caverns located deeper underground still. The one hovel was used for food storage, such that they did share all their spoils from fetching so that none was in want. The other was employed as a large meeting space for the entire network of small colonies for special gatherings, such as amusements, decisions on food sharing and work rotas, or so that they might merely renew their kinship one with the other lest they become estranged. The entire settlement was wholly underground and was discerned only with difficulty from the surface, being hidden from friend and foe alike.

And no rules were etched on their cell walls. Yet, all the colonies gathered in the underground meeting cavern, where principles of conduct were devised deftly over days of deliberation and debate. These beliefs were publicly recited in unison by all. Vows were made to abide by them with mind and heart and antenna. Otherwise, ants could think and speak and do as their own whimsy advised, with no ant holding an antenna over the head of another. Every ant memorized and agreed to these ten precepts.

All ants shall personally and daily seek
the unseen Pale White Ant's counsel.
All ants shall put to memory the Chronicles of Entgora.

All ants are equal.
All ants shall work.
All ants are free-thinkers and free-doers.
Ants shall not have an evilish eye.
Ants shall not fib.
Ants shall not pilfer.
Ant shall not kill ant.
Ants shall not smear their
faces with white or any other hue.

Imprisonment and putting to death of transgressors were not practices to be found amongst them. Ants that did not abide by the community tenets were reprimanded for a first offence and for a time were given extra work duties determined by their colony. After a second wrongdoing, they were shunned for some days, given extra work duties, and also required to make appropriate restitution where possible to the offended ant. Ultimately, one was banished forever from the colonies for a third crime, though this was like unto a great affliction of the heart and mind for all. And much lamentation and weeping would be made for the son or daughter of perdition.

Such was the strange and sad end of Trixter. Once a happy and playful ant in his youth, he became dour of soul soon after the great purging of Old Entgora. His wings had been bitten clean off by a group of Queen Entvladarka's raiding Shouters, who then took advantage of his weakness to beset him with other abuses too ghastly to recount.

Though he embraced the message of the Pale White Ant and had become an active member of the new settlement, he harboured a deep and secret bitterness of heart. Envy grew each time he saw other males make use of their wings to complete their daily chores, but especially when they would fly solely for pleasure's sake. Envy begat bitterness, and bitterness begat wrath. This hollow wound he fed with all manner of darkish thoughts until it became his only true companion, which he oft called "Dearest."

Not even to the Pale White Ant did he appeal privately to salve his injury. Then evil thought begat evil action. His first open offence was that of fibbing about completing his work duties; his second was thievery, when he pinched another male's daily food allotment. And for these he was fittingly disciplined according to community rule.

Yet this did not turn him from his wicked course, for at the opportune time his "Dearest" found him out and his rage at being chastised drove him to slay the one from whom he had pilfered. After being formally banished with the words "Get thee hence!" he was taken outside and watched by a large group of colonists as he walked off into the distance. As he reached just beyond eye view of his former home and the grieving but determined onlookers, he turned his head towards them with a defiant and twisted glare, vowing revenge and shouting a most vile curse. Yet he was not to be seen in the land again. No ant knows what fate he met. And Trixter was from that day forth recounted in antlore only by the name Grimface.

Now Gazer and her fellow citizens also appointed no Queen, had no ruling council of Reckoners, and elected no Proxies. No likenesses of supposedly important and influential ants were engraved on the walls. Even when Gazer was proposed by some to become Queen of all the colonies, she declined and reminded them of the true meaning of the words *equality, freedom,* and *unity.* Each colony was self-governing on day-to-day matters so that no one colony could interfere with the internal affairs of another. And each was small enough that making decisions by consensus was not too burdensome.

Sometimes a few pesky gabby ants would take advantage of the chance to listen to the pleasantness of their own voices. One of the most infamous offenders, Chatterchops, was forever and a day stringing together her most fanciful and unrelated ideas with "And suddenly…" or perhaps "And by the by…" or, when she was especially vigorous, "And now dearies, I tell you on my very own honour…"

Sometimes petty quarrels even arose about smidgens and specks and trifles and tidbits, especially among some of the males. In due course, though, a decision was taken. On the whole, all were happy because all voices were heard and all voted directly on all matters.

And their means to steward life and death were different than heretofore when they dwelt in the lands of the north. Concerning breeding, no longer were all females save one kept in barrenness, as was still the habit amongst the Old and New Entgorans who required and desired a Queen. But all females were free to birth hatchlings with their chosen lifelong male mate as their age, strength, and desire permitted.

Though this was such a new thing amongst them that, at the first, lifelong bonding appeared quite unseemly and unnatural, this arrangement eventually become most congenial to them with the evident benefits of affection and security.

The hatchlings that sprang forth were reared chiefly by their mother and father, but with the great assistance of their own colony. If a youngster strayed outside or accidentally wandered into one of the other colonies, none were in any wise gripped in worry, such was the watchfulness and tenderness of all full grown ants toward the young.

Some males and females did not seek mates nor breed, having given themselves solely to work, being possessed of an inner fire that bade them to serve the settlement without distraction but with single-mindedness. Among these were Gazer, Tenspeed, and Digdirt. Now, with regard to ants who died of oldishness or disease or injury, they were not heaped upon some rubbish pile as was the antish practice in the days of yore. Each was given burial as befitting an ant of this new order. A common grave site was in eye view of each colony in which the body of the dearly departed was carefully placed in its own small earthy chamber, supplications were made to the Pale White Ant to receive such one into her bosom, and a simple feast was given in which woe and lament were tempered with cheery song and fond remembrance. They grieved not as those who had no hope in the world.

And it came to pass during those early seasons of the settlement, that a popular song was heard from many a jowl and was entitled "Bellywonk's Lullaby," named after the oldish male ant who crafted the tune. It came first to be sung in this way.

One day, on his return flight home from a food rummage on the outside, Bellywonk noticed a little male hatchling sitting by himself under the shade of a rock, weeping softly. Upon inquiring as to what was troubling him, Bellywonk was told by the youngster, named Smallstride, that his friends no longer wanted to play with him because of the oddly way he spoke and because of his hobbledehoy manner. His left jaw was twisted from an accident at birth that caused him to make strange noises, the others teasing him with the name Buckjaw.

"And now," Smallstride cried, "my friends leaved me *click-a-shlick* and called me weird *click-a-shlick* and that they don't wants to play gameses with me never ever no more *click-a-shlick*." At the last *click-a-shlick*, he burst into heaving sobs.

"Laddy," Bellywonk assured him, "don't ye pay any mind to those that speak calumny of ye, for in this world there will be many of such mean-spirited disposition. Don't ye quail now, but rather withstand them and their assaults by bringing to your remembrance the Pale White Ant. And how she feared not to be different than others by doing a thing un-antlike and original and new, just so she would be true to herself and her dreams and those she loved. And here we are today because of her! Being different can be a good thing, for it means there is no other ant like ye in the whole wide world! It means ye are truly special!"

And then Bellywonk wiped the tears from little Smallstride's eyes and sang to him this jolly song, not noticing that the youngster slipped into peaceful slumber halfway through.

> *Come young and old, come one and all*
> *If ye are feeling sad*
> *And I will tell ye of the secret*
> *Of an ant so gladly glad*
>
> *If ye wiggle wiggle*
> *The antennae on your head*
> *It surely hardly matters*
> *What the other ants have said*
>
> *Just wiggle waggle woggle them*
> *With all your pow'r and might*
> *Before too long ye'll see*
> *That everything will be set right*
>
> *For being different means you're you*
> *And no one else but you*
> *Just stand up tall and get to work*
> *For there is much to do*
>
> *So lift that load and twist that twig*
> *And fetch that food for all*
> *Help build our home, ye young and old*
> *The future to us calls*

And old Bellywonk fashioned other songs that became well-loved by young and old alike, such as "Twig-a-Jig-Jig," "The Battle Hymn of Pangaea," "O Bonny Days for Ye and Me," and "Worker Ants Unite." And he would be oft invited to recite his newest words to the colonies when they gathered as one in the large underground meeting cavern, or as he travelled from colony to colony. To his delight, not a few youths asked to become his learners, including Smallstride, to whom he taught the skill of songcraft. And he became affectionately known as the Old Minstrel or the Old Wonk.

For a long spell, the colonies had not yet considered what they might call themselves, for it was but a small matter. Then one day, during a meeting of the entire network of small colonies, Ponderella proposed that they name themselves "The Voluntary Association of Leaderless, Underground, Small-sized, Self-governing, Non-violent Ant Colonies." All agreed that though this idea was well devised and described them well, it was too cumbersome a thing for some ants to speak or remember. Then the always amusing and well-meaning Wagwit realized that if the first antish character of each word was strung together, a new word was formed: VALUSSNAC. But this made no sense to anyone, and some did not like the way it sounded. Now, being simple ants, they desired a simple name that even youngsters could understand. And so, the young hatchlings themselves crafted this name: Entopia. This was pleasing to all.

In this way did life carry on in Entopia for some seasons. And they did grow into a mighty company in numbers and in vigour.

12

the day of reckoning

Clouds rolled over the dark sky that afternoon. It had been a few seasons since the founding of New Entgora and Entopia. Although there was generally peace and good will between them, some New Entgorans were increasingly critical of the Entopians for being un-antlike in the way they organized their society. The Entopians were thought of as eccentric and traitors and were not expected to survive long. No Queen? No leaders? No army? No prominent anthill? No prisons?

Some New Entgorans put forward that perhaps the ants of Entopia might not even be real ants after all. And they were often disparagingly called Gazerites or Gazerenes or, worst of all, Gazerants, all names that Gazer disliked because of the unwanted fame it gave to one ant, namely her, at the expense of recognizing the toil of others. "Fey! Folly!" she would scowl each time she heard rumour of one of these names uttered in her presence.

Yet, a few curious inquirers from New Entgora would on occasion covertly visit the Entopians, some even forsaking their old way of life to become its new citizens. And although the civil war was still fiery and ongoing in Old Entgora, a grudging respect developed between old Queen Entvladarka and the rebel leader Cruncher, having seen something of themselves in each other.

Not surprisingly, Old Entgorans were unaware even of the existence of Entopia.

One day, a trio of friends from New Entgora was fetching food to the far west of their home. Anything would do. Small bits of fruit. A moist seed. A puddle of water. As they scavenged, one of them noticed an odd smell borne by the western wind and mentioned it to her companions. They stopped and surveyed the air with their wiggling antennae, moving their heads in all directions.

"Come, let's lay eyes on it," one of them said grimly.

They trotted quickly for some time in the direction of the sour scent. Suddenly, they came to a halt as they hit a wall of their own fear. They dug their feet into the dirt to steady themselves. They were staring into the familiar face of doom. They were now staring at the approaching Blue Grey Hordes. All three of the ants had fought some seasons ago in the Second War of the West and knew the swift destruction of this enemy. And they also knew that the only chance they had of survival were the combined forces of Old Entgora, New Entgora, and Entopia. As they ran back east, they diverged one from the other, each heading to one of the three settlements of Entgoran ants to warn them of the impending danger.

The first ant to sound the warning was the one who reached her own New Entgora. Her compatriots were quick to respond to the alarming words of one of their own and mobilized their entire population to war. Most streamed out of the anthill and gathered to the west, while several hundreds filled the trenches that surrounded their home to make a last stand.

The second ant then reached Old Entgora. The Queen's sentinels took the advancing ant—by this time shouting out ghastly warnings—into captivity and interrogated her as to whether she was a spy sent by the New Entgorans or whether she be one of Cruncher's rebels lurking about. At the last, they believed the terrible report and sounded the call to war. But the forces of old Queen Entvladarka and the insurgent Cruncher did not trust the other and would not fight side by side as one army but gathered as two separate columns outside the anthill. The aged Queen's army numbered in the many tens of thousands, while the rebel army was one-third in might. As with all antish wars, both Old and New Entgoran settlements left some elder ants inside their anthills to mind young hatchlings and eggs.

The third messenger was the last to reach her secluded destination, which she found with some effort, as Entopia was fully underground. She traced the familiar Entgoran ant scent until she happened upon a cluster of ants going about their tasks quietly, moving in and out through holeways in the ground. The messenger identified herself as a New Entgoran and announced to the ants that the Blue Grey Hordes were advancing. She pleaded with her audience to take her inside so their colony could be warned and rallied to war.

The Entopians told the messenger that they vowed to do no harm to other ants, even if they themselves were in danger. "Ant shall not kill ant," they asserted. But the bearer of bad tidings begged until they relented and was whisked into the large meeting hollow deep below, where soon the entire network of colonies was gathered. Many hundreds were assembled.

After the noise died down, one of the Entopians named Wiggler spoke. "Sisters, greetings and peace to you all in the name of the Pale White Ant! Her coming is near! As some of you have already become aware, grave danger approaches from the west. A visitor from New Entgora brings us dark tidings. Friend, please speak your mind freely."

"Greetings to you from New Entgora!" began Runner. "Thank you for your kindnesses and hospitality. Friends, as my comrades and I were searching for food far west of our home, the wind spoke to us of a foul stench. We moved towards it to find out what it was. Then we saw it. We thought we were staring into the face of death itself. I bring you dire news. Friends, the Blue Grey Hordes are once again advancing from the west!"

Murmurs of dismay swept over part of the meeting. But many of the ants were undisturbed by these words and remained calm.

"Friend, what would you have us do?" asked Clickmouth meekly.

"As we speak, Old and New Entgora are mobilizing for open war against the foe," added Runner. "If antkind in the east is to survive, we must band together to ward off this common enemy. I have come not just to warn you, but also to summon you into battle alongside the other Entgoran settlements."

"We Entopians are a group of small colonies," injected Feeler. "We have not much might. We number only in the hundreds and do not have the strength of even one legion. We cannot sway the outcome of this war."

"Every wiggling antenna," chirped Runner, "every twitching leg, every living ant can make a difference if we unite. We must stave off this evil. Let us unite to bring peace to our lands!" Runner now wondered why the obvious was unclear to her audience. Perhaps they had become feebleminded from all these seasons apart from true civilization.

"Sisters," began Gazer, who was listening intently to the discussion, "our visitor's words carry the truth. We are well acquainted with the dangers of tyrants and armies. Most here lived through the days of the great purge in Old Entgora, when the long evil antenna of Queen Entvladarka bullied and butchered and banished many thousands. Most of us also, except the younglings of course, fought in the Second War of the West against the Hordes and remember the fierceness of

102

this foe. They were bigger and stronger and swifter than we. And we gave them fight and somehow survived. Yes, we all know well the dangers of tyrants and armies.

"But, sisters, lest we forget, let us remember that we established our colonies after their fashion in order to flee the cruelty and ego and greed of Queens and councils, leaders and masters, all lords of destruction. We sojourn here to create a new society of equality, freedom, and unity, so that a new ant might be hatched that will rise from the dust and stride peacefully over the earth and follow in the path of the Pale White One. We are ants of non-violence and have lived these many days according to one of our most sacred sayings, 'Ant shall not kill ant.'

"We shall not repay evil with evil, but we will repay evil with good. For those who live by violence, shall die in violence. Deal kindly with your aggressors, that they may be swayed from their evil course. We are in this world, but not of it. We are ants belonging to another realm. Therefore, we will not raise an angry antenna against a fellow ant, even to defend our very lives in war. For this is the way of the Pale One. Sisters, remember the prophecies. Vengeance shall be meted out against the destroyers of the earth and antkind in due time!"

Much of the congregation swayed and squeaked in agreement. But not all, for a small number differed sharply with Gazer's practical application of the proverb that prohibited ant killing.

"Wiggledy sticks!" cheeped Stoutface in disagreement. "I dispute Gazer's understanding of our sayings. Surely, the adage 'Ant shall not kill ant' does not apply in this case. We must defend our colonies against the reckless hate of the Hordes. Shall we stand idly by while evil sweeps over us and drowns us in its malice? Shall we stand idly by while young hatchlings are murdered before they even have a chance to glimpse their futures? Shall we stand idly by while our elder ants are chased down and trodden underfoot? Shall we stand idly by while the sweat and tears that built our new society are mingled with our own blood? Surely not! While we wait for the prophesied days of peace to come and the return of the Great Pale One, we live in this world and must be part of it. Otherwise, we are false to each other and are traitors to our heritage and our future. This is a just war. This is a holy cause. This hour of need beckons to all who would hear. Sisters, I go now with Runner to lay down my life for you. Who else will come with me?"

From all over the hollow, antennae here and there were raised with loud hollers of "I will!" and "Let's go to the fight!"

"Sisters, indeed," whistled Tenspeed over the noise, "our colonies, truly, truly, are free societies. All here know that all are free to follow their consciences. Remember our saying, 'All ants are free-thinkers and free-doers.' This hour, this very hour, is no exception. We wish you to reconsider sister Gazer's wisely words, though, and the warnings and the outcomes of your actions. And I can both see and hear that most of you agree. She is in the right. She is in the right. I say it openly. But none here are your masters or leaders and, no, no, not even your Queens. So, at the last, at the very last, you ants who wish to go with Stoutface and Runner to the battle have that liberty."

And so one of ten ants, some seventy in total, clustered round the two vocal proponents of the war, who then led them out of the grand hollow. They were accompanied by pleadings to reconsider. Others said they would ask the Pale One to protect them.

But all wept openly at the departure of their friends. The Entopians remained together and began a long vigil, calling on the Pale One for shelter and wisdom and courage. All the while Gazer's mind was busy a-plotting.

As Runner, Stoutface, and the seventy reached the battlefront, they arrived to see hundreds of thousands of ants now ready for bloodshed, some to expand their realms and some to defend them. A mighty host had assembled. The Blue Grey Hordes of Entmerika were at a standstill some distance away and faced in the direction of the three columns of black ants arrayed against them under the separate commands of Entvladarka, Cruncher, and Whistler.

Envoys were sent for a crisis meeting to be arranged far behind the battle lines of the Entgoran commander-in-chiefs to conjure a stratagem. After much effort and slander and many a curse, they were able to conquer their mutual ill will and decide on a common course. An emissary of three ants, one from each of the armies, was to be sent to herald a message to the Queen of the Entmerikan Blue Grey Hordes. After the old antish fashion, the three worker ants walked side by side toward the foe's frontline with antennae entwined, showing both their unity and peaceful intent.

As they approached the rival army, the three were stunned to see that many black ants—former Entgorans who were taken captive during the Second War of the West, or so they thought—were sprinkled all along the frontline of the enemy. It was like a dazzling and shimmering wave of speckled blue and grey and black. When they reached the vanguard, the tightly packed Horde army parted down the middle, allowing the emissaries to pass through and just as quickly closed ranks again, which looked to the Entgoran armies as if their compatriots had been swallowed alive by some beastly beast.

Alas, no harm beset them, and they passed in safety until they were face to face with the Queen of the Hordes. They could see she was much larger and fatter and hairier—and to them more hideous—than any of their own Queens or commanders. She made a constant sniffing sound and a streak of saliva drizzled down her left jaw. And the sour stench of the Horde warriors—grander also in stature than the average Entgoran fighters—was overpowering to the three envoys.

"Haaalt!" the Queen growled. "Stooop yooor steeeps rrright

theeer leeetle ones!" The Queen had a way of stretching out her words. To the messengers, it sounded unnecessary, unpleasant, and uncivilized. Whether this way of antspeak was common among the Entmerikan army was uncertain, for they remained deadly quiet. "Yeee come in truuus, I seee! Ha! Speeek it quikleee!"

"Greetings to you, Queen of Entmerika!" began one of the message bearers harshly. "We come with tidings from our leaders. This is their message: 'Greetings, mighty Queen of Entmerika. We the three Queens of the Entgorans are united and act as one. We are fierce and fearless. We are swift and sly. We are mighty and many. You have two choices. Either turn back from whence you came and live, or continue on your present course and be vanquished this very day.' "

The message was wrathful and crafted with care. Queen Entvladarka knew from experience that Entmerikans only respected those that opposed them openly and boldly. Peradventure, the Hordes might retreat, not from fear, but rather from high opinion of the foe. Queens Cruncher and Whistler both agreed to this contrivance. The Entmerikan monarch mused over the words spoken to her for some time, turning them over in her mind, all the while making distasteful sniffing and gurgling sounds, cackling to herself on occasion.

She suddenly loomed over the hapless trio—who shrank back startled—and snarled, wildly waving her long antennae and forelegs threateningly. "Ha! I scofff at yooor Queeens. They are weeek and wretched. Smaaall and pitiful. Yooor antkind was conquered in the laaast war. And maaany of yooor ants now fight in my arrrmy. My realm weeel grrrow theees day. Sooo, let yooor pooorrr foolish Queeens come against meee. Tell yooor Queeens this: 'Ha! I am the mighty Queeen of Entmerrrika, and weee are the only grand power in theees lands. The antsss of the east weeel fall. Theees day I weeel see yooor very heads dangle and decorate my private chambers.

106

Eeef I had not eaten alrrready, I would even swallow the thrrree of yeee whole this very hour. Ha!' Now, be gone! Off with yeee! Ha!"

The messengers scampered off hastily, retracing their route through the gaping mouth of the parting Horde army back to their own. They crossed over the dusty but clean patch of ground a thousand ants wide between the opposing armies—now in scorn called No Ant's Land by some of the older soldiery—where they would come to their clash. They returned to the still gathered Queens and delivered the Entmerikan message.

It was clear and displeasing to all that fight would come upon them soon. The three Queens trotted back to their positions far behind the frontlines. The Entmerikans of the west and the Entgorans of the east stiffened their bodies, dug their feet into the dirt, and readied themselves to redden the ground. A mighty host had assembled. The hour of reckoning had come. The Third War of the West was now upon them. "In the name of the Queens! Ants advance!" came the cry from the Engorans. "To war! Crush the foe!" came the call from the Entmerikans. Both armies marched slowly at first, picking up their pace and soon rushing at full speed.

From far and away out of the southeast, to everyone's astonishment, a trio of ants suddenly rushed into the middle of No Ant's Land. It was Digdirt, Tenspeed, and Gazer, come from Entopia. Whether it was to still the madness or to wage war, all were unsure. But the armies rushed on, unswayed.

"Well, dear friends," Digdirt said to her companions with a confident grin, as she turned to survey the approaching armies while vigorously scratching the ground, "here we are in the midst of a time not of our making. A time that belongs to the bold!"

"And what a time it is!" added Tenspeed. "I daresay, if my mind still be as sharp and my eyes be as keen as ever, me myself thinks that the hour has come for her to arise. But these armies cannot, surely will not, stop their cruel cruelness and mad madness now. Oh, higgledy piggledy! My fear, truly, indeed, is that perhaps Entopia has failed in its purpose."

Gazer thought for a brief moment and smiled mischievously, studying closely the faces of her two friends. She was glad to have known Digdirt, the one who saved her life in the last war and who always showed immense braveliness. Gazer also harkened back to the first time Tenspeed and she played bury-and-hunt when they were but hatchlings. While Tenspeed counted to forty in her own hurried way, Gazer scurried off to dig the hole in which she planned to hide the agreed-upon pebble of great price, a ruddy, shiny, smooth stone. She ran so recklessly that she tripped head-over-feet, tossed the pebble straight up into the air, and somersaulted into a line of marching Shouters, felling the entire lot. The pebble came plummeting down onto Gazer's head. *Plonk!* The memory of that sound jolted Gazer back into reality and the present menace they faced.

"These are murky days," Gazer began, "and the minds of ants are wrapped in shadow. Indeed, we ourselves may not see the dawn with our own eyes. And we may not have accomplished all we were meant to. But these things matter not. For if company is true and we have been loyal to the Pale One, then victory will surely come in due time." Then with a twinkle in her eyes and recalling her hatchling days of play, Gazer added, "Sisters, to the dance!"

At this, the trio entwined forelegs, danced slowly around in a circle, and sang a new song so loudly that the quickly approaching armies could not help but hear.

The circle is unbroken
If company is true
The path remains untrodden

108

Till walked on by the few
The ants of old Pangaea
From evil shall not cease
The Great One flares her jowls
And chants her hymn of peace

The Entmerikans and Entgorans charged at each other and clashed in the middle of No Ant's Land, crushing and trampling the trio to death and splattering their blood.

Theirs was the first blood spilt in this conflict, the Third War of the West. Digdirt, Tenspeed, and Gazer had fallen and come to their end of days.

Since the last conflict between these ant tribes in the Second War of the West, they had grown in number and experience and ferocity, weapons that made this contest all the more dreadful. The Entgoran Queens dispatched commands and manoeuvres from the far rear near the Hill of Fatgrass, while the Entmerikan monarch did the same on the edge of No

Ant's Land close to the Waters of Darktree. No longer were their regal eyes set on mere survival or victory, but the complete annihilation of the other, even if the cost was their own extinction. Mutual ant destruction. Deep was their malice and malevolence, more so than they themselves had realized before the struggle began.

The Entgoran Queens gave the command, "Jaws of Death!" using the same tactic as in the previous war with the foe, retreating a column of Queen Entvladarka's Old Entgorans through the middle to the east to tempt the Entmerikans into the centre. A second mass of Queen Entvladarka's forces circled north, while Queens Cruncher and Whistler moved their troops south. Their aim was to rendezvous in the centre and crush the Entmerikans in their gigantic jaw-like contrivance. But the Blue Grey warriors split into northern and southern columns that pushed wide the Entgoran jaws of death, sending a column of their black slave ants to give chase through the middle.

The black Entmerikans did not defect to fight for the black Entgorans—as Queen Entvladarka hoped—but were fanatically loyal to the Entmerikan ruler, having been bred from the original Entgoran slave conscripts obtained in the last war. Black ant now fought black ant, giving the Entmerikan Queen great pleasure at the irony.

The northern column of Entmerikans drove the Old Entgorans north of their home, giving them fight with mighty bite, jaw to jaw, out on the open plain. Many heads and antennae and legs on both sides were savagely severed, leaving still-twitching body parts strewn across the expanse of land as food for the beasts.

To the south, hundreds of New Entgorans were thrust by the stronger and swifter enemy into the water trench encircling their home, there plunging into their watery grave, drowning in full view of their terrified comrades on the other side of the trough. Other New Entgorans were pushed as far south as the Exodus Tree, there fighting the Blue Grey swarm ant to ant inside, outside, atop, and under it and filling its hollow with the enemy's dead bodies. Here the New Entgorans made good advantage of their familiarity with the tree.

Then, quite suddenly, a loud *thump, thump, thump!* from the east was heard by the ants waging battle north of Old Entgora. Charging across the Field of Yellowgrass and trampling the Bloodflower came three large Longtails to the terror of all. With their hard and rough skin—speckled black and grey and white—their sharp-clawed feet, and their long tails—about half the length of their entire bodies—the beasts scraped their bellies across the ground as they ran toward the screaming ants. With gaping mouths and lunging blue tongues, hundreds of ants were swept up into the chomping jaws and gulping gullets of these cruel creatures. The fiends relished in their foul feast, trampling many underfoot as they moved around in pursuit of their scurrying prey.

The order then came from the Entmerikan Queen, "My daughterrrs, swarrrm theeez brooots!" one of which soon found itself covered from head to tail in thousands of vengeful ant warriors, all biting and chomping at its eyes and softer patches of skin. The Longtail finally toppled over dead under the fury of its assailants. But the other two succeeded in shaking off the attacking swarms and continued their feeding frenzy.

And at the same time, from out of the deep southwest, bounded three large Outside Beasts. *Thud, thud, thud!* They rushed towards and interrupted the ant war being waged in and around the Exodus Tree. These were the beasts of legend and song. These were the creatures that filled ant dreams with vile images for many a generation. These were the scourges of antkind.

The Outside Beasts were hundreds of ants tall and a thousand ants long, from the tip of their long thin mouths to the end of their long bushy tails. Covered all over with thick strong hair, they trod heavily upon the earth with their four wide clawed feet. Two of the beasts moved quickly to each side of the Exodus Tree to hinder any ants from escaping, slurping up countless victims with their long thin tongues. The third rolled the hollow tree to and fro with both its forelegs while sticking its tongue repeatedly into holes in the bark of the tree, pulling into its hungry mouth many screaming ants—both Entmerikans and Entgorans.

Then it began. *Plop, plop, plop!* A few at first. Then a few more. The dry dust of the ground began drinking in falling drops of water under a cloudy sky. Then the sky opened up and released a torrent of rain. The ground swelled with water, sweeping much of the entire region clean of all ant life. And the Waters of Darktree overflowed, sending floodwaters towards Old Entgora and taking thousands of warring ants to their deaths.

Many tried to escape the wet doom by climbing up the side of the anthills or racing to the top of the Stone of Greenwood or the Exodus Tree, but they were all too easily washed away. The force of the rain was so strong as to even damage greatly beyond repair the anthills of Old and New Entgora, destroying the elder ants and hatchlings that were inside. No Ant's Land was true to its name. As the sky flish-flashed with lightning and crickle-crackled with thunder, it frightened away the Longtails and Outside Beasts to search for shelter. The rain drenched the earth for forty hours.

And after the last raindrop plummeted to the ground, the Entopian colonies emerged from their secrecy. During the great rainfall, they thrust large balls of dirt to plug the holeways that led to the ground surface, so as to thwart the waters from flooding into their underground mazework. The dry dirt plugs were now wet mud. The ants burrowed through with some struggle, like a butterfly freeing itself from its cocoon. Drippy drops of water seeped through some of the pierced holeways, washing over the ants forcefully, but to no harm's end. As they dug their feet into the muck and mire and gazed into the distance, they could hear and see and smell no sign of ongoing warfare. The conflict was over. But even the rain could not sweep away the smell of death wafting through the air.

The colonies trudged slowly through the sticky ground to the battlefields, with the aim of collecting the dead and with the faint hope of discovering survivors. They divided into six companies of a goodly hundred ants each, being charged with the care of certain sectors of the landscape.

As they swept northwest, they were aghast at the sight of hundreds of thousands of dead antkind strewn across the entire region. Blood. Bodies. Severed and crushed heads, antennae, and legs. Ants afloat in pools of water. Many fallen combatants were found clustered together and heaped on top of one other. Others were alone in their deaths. The limbs of some foes were still locked in conflict, even as the warriors met their watery end. Red blood and brown mud now mingled with the blue, grey, and black skin of the ants themselves. The white painted faces of Old Entgoran Shouters were seen here and there.

The scattered dead were piled together at the three main battlefields—signs of which were even now manifest to any ant with a keenly attuned antenna—to the north of Old Entgora, near the Exodus Tree, and east of No Ant's Land just south of Old Entgora. And the bodies of the Entmerikan Horde Queen and the three Entgoran Queens were found and heaped onto the mounds of the dead, but no more ceremoniously than any other. The winged flying beasties of prey would surely come to cleanse the land of all ant carcasses, these dreadful monuments of an age that would soon pass into distant memory.

A smallish number of survivors, though, both Entgorans and Entmerikans, were found wounded and close to their end. These were borne on the backs of their rescuers far southeast to Entopia to be nursed back to life. And the ants toiled and grieved for many an hour until their mission was accomplished, returning wearily home.

Then a lone loud whistle of lament shot out from the wilderness of No Ant's Land. A small cadre of Entopian ants still scavenging far west had stumbled upon the mangled remains of their fallen sisters, still bound together in their dance. Anguish jolted through their limbs, tempered only by the joyful remembrances of the valiant Digdirt, the enchanting Tenspeed, and the wise Gazer. Reverently, their bodies were hoisted aloft and marched home in long procession.

114

When they arrived, the entire population of Entopia hastily emerged aboveground to greet them with a mixture of glad and mournful weeping and chirping and cheeping and clickity-clacking. In full view of all, the three champions were buried just east of the colonies. Twelve stones marked their common grave. All knew that the prophecies had come to pass.

And a grand hymn was devised and sung by three disciples of Bellywonk—the Old Wonk—who had come to his end of days peacefully while asleep during the night, shortly before the war began.

> *The Third War of the West didst blow*
> *Like wind across the earth*
> *And brought the fate of all antkind*
> *Unto the Pale One's myrth*
> *Selah, selah*
>
> *The Blue Grey Hordes of foulest stench*
> *Were led by fouler Queen*
> *And hurled great vengeance, hate, and death*
> *At all their foes unseen*
> *Selah, selah*
>
> *Though Old and New Entgoran clans*
> *Didst not flee but gave fight*
> *Their mighty stratagems and ploys*
> *Couldst not thrust fiends to flight*
> *Selah, selah*
>
> *The malice and malevolence*
> *That blemisheth antkind*
> *Didst bring upon them judgments three*
> *For future ants a sign*
> *Selah, selah*

The first great wroth of Longtails came
With hungry bluish tongues
The second of the Outside Beast
Didst fell both old and young
Selah, selah

The third didst pierce the sky, which bled
A mighty torrent rain
To all the ruthless tribes of war
A potent final bane
Selah, selah

Entopians with noble cause
Danced jigs and sang of peace
Yet Gazer, Tenspeed, and Digdirt
Were trod by antish beasts
Selah, selah

The foretellings of oldish lore
Have come to stake their claim
The Great White Ant returns unseen
And brings her holy reign
Selah, selah

For the benefit of future generations this was later added to the Chronicles of Entgora, to the pleasure of all. The Entopian colonies were also now populated by former Entmerikans and Old and New Entgorans who had survived the war. Having experienced the kindliness and teachings of Entopia and observing the way of life therein, they gladly became its newest citizens. Females and males, workers and soldiers, Entmerikans and Entgorans were now all one. They all toiled and feasted and celebrated side by side with full equality, freedom, and unity, with neither a Queen nor master in sight. Old things were passing beyond memory, for new things had come. And the reign of the unseen Pale White One—the Great Ant—descended over them all.

And there was peace in the land for an age.

about the author

RAD ZDERO obtained his Ph.D. degree in Mechanical Engineering from Queen's University (Kingston, Canada), specializing in orthopaedic biomechanics. He is currently the director of a hospital-based orthopaedic biomechanics research lab. He enjoys epic walks, coffee shops, books, movies, music, towns with obscure architecture, and peaceful revolutions.

Readers are invited to contact the author to discuss *Entopia: Revolution of the Ants*.

Rad Zdero
P.O. Box 39528
Lakeshore P.O.
Mississauga, ON
Canada L5G-4S6
Email: rzdero@yahoo.ca

Printed in the United States
103227LV00002B/1-48/A